The Shepherd's Daughter

by

Nicolette Jinks

Paperback Edition OCTOBER 2014
ISBN 978-0-9857210-2-2

You may contact the author via email: nicolette.jinks@gmail.com or check in at Facebook, Google+, or GoodReads. To follow the author, her blog is www.nicolettejinks.wordpress.com, where she writes about writing and life.

A Standal Publications Book
Independently Published by author doing business as
Standal Publications
393 River Road
Bliss, Idaho 83314

www.theblackkettlecafe.wordpress.com

The Shepherd's Daughter

by

Nicolette Jinks

STANDAL PUBLICATIONS

Dedication

To my family,

for tolerating my obsession with unicorns for so many
years, and giving me so many books on the theme.

A Note from the Author

As a child, I always had great difficulty sleeping and so my parents gave me great stacks of books and a flashlight to read at night after everyone else had fallen asleep. It did not take long for fantasy creatures, particularly unicorns and dragons, to completely overtake my imagination.

Though I do not see the theme as frequently now as I remember, there was usually either a scene or a reference in the unicorn stories to a virgin girl luring in the unicorns. Sometimes this would start a partnership between unicorn and girl, but other times, the unicorn would lay his head in her lap and then be slain by a hunter who was standing guard. As a child who adored all animals, this naturally appalled me. But what it did even more was inspire questions.

Why hunt a unicorn? Why did it have to be a girl to lure in the creature? Why a virgin? This was important because if she wasn't a virgin, she faced death from the unicorn. What did the unicorn even want with a virgin, anyhow? Even in my innocence, this smacked of both religious undertones and sexuality.

One day, I listened to a short story which addressed unicorn hunting, and all this came back to my memory. Some research later, I discovered articles discussing virginity in the medieval ages detailing how being a virgin was considered a career and lifelong pursuit wherein women had their time freed from fulfilling a husband's desires and caring for children. These women could read and devote themselves to a holy life. Thus my tendril of a tale suddenly *had* to include significant doses of religion. While I try to avoid such topics out of sensitivity, I found that to ignore it completely would be dishonest.

The Shepherd's Daughter started at only 7,000 words, but to explore the story properly, it has grown to its current length of 70,000 words. Hope you enjoy it.

Nicolette

CHAPTER 1

It was not Sunday, least of all an important one, yet a neighbor had spoken to Father, urging him to report to the King's men which of his daughters were eligible for the sacrifice. My eldest sister and I went with him into town. She, to buy wedding slippers; and me, to be removed from squabbling with far too many sisters older and younger than I.

"I'm old enough," I reminded him when he revealed his mission on the road just outside the village. "But you can't let Mary or Sarah enter. They'd go all callahooa if they had to leave home."

My oldest sister giggled. Father paused under the branches of an elm to study me and brush the dust off his tunic. "Callahooa, Melody?"

I lowered my voice. "That's what happens when you see a ghost."

Father glanced at Allie as we made our way into town. She'd been smiling more and more the closer the wedding date came, and she left home sometimes after my parents had fallen asleep, to talk with her betrothed. I kept her secret. She said, "It means crazy, Father."

"Your sisters are callahooa enough without enduring strife. You two alone inherited all my sensibilities." He paused while we fell to victim to preening at his praise, then he added, "And my talents, but I fear only one of you is old enough to understand what those are."

My sister nodded. I did, too, of course, thinking of his patience and uncanny way with animals.

We entered the village, a place with narrow streets and lots of smoke wafting out of chimneys, a place where bread baked all day and not just for supper. Father's eyes darkened and he stopped his absent-minded chewing of a piece of willow bark, assuming his serious thinking face which always made my stomach churn. Who had done something wrong this time?

From our vantage at the corner of the village's only inn and tavern, we could fully view the public square just outside the church's cemetery. There was a great, silent crowd crushed in around the pillory; this confused me a great deal, since last time a man had been taken there for nakedness, there had been a mass of loud voices and even some rotten cabbages thrown at him. Pillory was a place where people beat you while you had your head and ankles latched into holes in a wooden board, not a place where loved ones stood guard alongside.

It was then that I saw the King's men in bright scarlet in front of the town hall, swords hanging at their hips, arms crossed. I saw one of Allie's friends, a girl who never did anything wrong, shivering in the cool shadow of the square, having been given one of the boards that takes wrists and ankles instead of the neck. My stomach shrank. "Father, why is Ruth there?"

Allie grabbed me by the shoulders and tried to hide my face in her skirts, but I yanked away from her indignantly. Father still hadn't answered, and we had drawn the attention of the King's men.

"Why is Ruthie in the stocks?" I demanded, my voice louder this time.

"She is a sinner, child," came a stranger's voice.

I spun, coming face to waist with a monk's brownish-black robes, one from the black sheep, undyed. Father got a lot for their wool. I bristled and spat at the intruding monk, "You don't know her! You don't know any of us. How can you say she's a sinner?"

True, deep silence coated the public square, a quietness which rarely happened out in the meadows where lambs seldom stopped playing; I felt disapproving eyes peering down on me. Unconcerned, the monk said, "I know because she told me she was. She said she was unwed, and ineligible to be a sacrifice. She is a fallen woman, and they are taken to the pillory."

My face heated, and I wanted to reply when my father's smooth voice said, "Or, perhaps, she would rather face the stocks than risk enlistment in the King's service."

"It is sin to lie."

Father inclined his head. "Perhaps people fear more for their lives than their souls. I presume there is a charitable contribution offered to buy absolution from these duties?"

While the monk gasped at Father like a dying fish, one of the King's men answered Father's question in soft tones. The monk, meanwhile, objected to the red-clothed man. "There ought not be a way to buy a name. Every eligible maiden should stand to attend with her head high for her services."

To which the sword-carrying man responded, "If gowns were free and meals were as well, I might take your stance. But securing the life of a virgin and keeping her safe from sin: That is a costly endeavor, and we have eligible maidens enough."

The monk turned and left, followed shortly after by the other man. Conversation, and weeping, as some of the relatives of those pilloried had started to cry, resumed at its usual muted level.

Father tapped his finger against his coin purse, his face the same distracted calculations I saw upon it when he didn't have enough to pay the tax man and buy wheat both. His gaze lifted to my sister. "If the village doesn't punish the girls, the lord's men will. You're to be married in three weeks. Can I buy Melody's name, or do I need to buy yours?"

She blushed, but I couldn't think of why. Frustration made me say, "No, I need to go. There's nothing here for me to do."

I was thinking of the not-so-nice ways the last tradeswoman had turned me down, and angrily resenting the good fortune of sisters who had found their trades or were too young to yet look.

"I promised your mother we would see Mistress Cotter. She may take you as a pupil if you show talent." But Father's thoughts weren't on me, they were on Allie. And Allie was staring at the pillory, her face drawn, pale, and her eyes wide in fear. I sensed, rather than heard,

Father's long sigh.

Father didn't say anything to us, or even to greet our neighbors and townsfolk, before he took long strides to the king's men, his shepherd's crook making light taps in the dust of the streets like a slow banging of a judge's gavel.

A needle jabbed through four layers of wool, pricking my finger. I let out a hiss and sucked the blood away, looking at the uneven stitches, the stray strands poking out of the hem, and the overall misshapen lump of fabric meant to be a pouch. Mother wouldn't be impressed; the sewing woman, Mistress Cotter, who did odd jobs would be even less likely than before to teach me her trade.

"Melody," Mother's voice warned me of her arrival, but I wasn't quick enough to hide what she would call a 'waste of good wool'. Nevertheless, when she stood in the doorway, the bucket of milk seemed to drag her arms down. She wasn't looking at what I was doing. She was looking at me as though it were the first and last time. "Put that nonsense down. Go outside. Lord Richmond has sent for you."

There was a hardness to her voice which wasn't showing in her face. I dropped the half-formed pouch onto the bench where we took supper, and realized that last night would be the last time I ate here, if I knew what Mother was saying. Excitement tore through my veins, but I had the sense to not show it. "They picked me? For the sacrifice?"

Mother's mouth went thin. She nodded. "Why

couldn't you be gifted with a common thing, like all your sisters?"

I bit my lip, determined to not let her see the sting of her words. Instead I motioned to the fabric, warning, "It's got a needle in it."

"Take it."

At first I didn't believe I'd heard her right—that was the best bone needle we had, and she had to know I was using it. Then I wondered if I was hearing her right from the very beginning. She stood with her back to me, but her hands were still and her back rigid.

"I said take it, Melody. You need to get going. Richmond's man won't wait."

I wasn't sure what to say. After all, yesterday I had been pining and sighing, upset to think that Lord Richmond had chosen a different virgin. It had been weeks since the pillories and the name-taking, and Allie's wedding was almost upon us. Mother had never told me what she thought on the matter, even as Father told me stories far into the night. Then I felt the lump of wool, and used it to wrap up the needle before tying it into my belt.

As I blinked in the morning light, I let my fingers linger on the mud and wattle of our home. I said, softly, "I'll make you proud."

Mother took in a breath. "I know."

The mud crumbled beneath my fingers, and I stepped away from the house, going for a small barn where I saw my sisters trying to hide and spy. Two girls shrieked when I walked up behind them, then they pointed around the edge of the barn, blocking my view entirely. I would be glad to be on my own, out from behind their silliness and breathy laughing.

"Girls, let Melody through," my father called. Often I denied sharing any characteristics with my sisters, and for the most part it was true.

My sisters stepped aside, pink cheeked, and I took several steps forward. The sun was well into the sky and early spring lambs napped in piles of dry hay which had fed their mothers. Our home itself was finally unshrouded from the billowy mist of drying rain, and the rank odors of lanolin and sheep poop were returning with the warming sun. That was the one good thing about winter: Nothing smelled. But the trade for spring was the coming pretty white edelweiss and snow drops, and the happy roar of engorged creeks and rivers. A nightingale sang when I passed the open to reach my father and the man in scarlet.

My eyes were lowered to the ground to avoid stepping barefoot in the cow's manure. I felt like a lamb being examined for quality, to decide if I should be kept or culled out of the flock. A stranger's voice made me raise my gaze.

"That is Melody? I have never taken one so young." His objections held no sway over my father, who had readied himself for weeks should this come to be. The stranger's horse gleamed in the sunlight, and his saddle bore the mark of the crown. The man stared at me, appealing to me this time. "Dragons eat little girls like you."

He was certainly thinking me a runt, but Father often stressed that size didn't make a good ewe. Everything else mattered more. Still, I glanced at the slender man leaning on a shepherd's crook, wearing a tattered cloak and giving me the same appraising expression that the noble was. Father had warned me I would face trials. If I wouldn't stand up to a sword man, how could I face a dragon? I shook my head. "Sheep are better, and we have been giving him the culls for centuries."

"Are you certain she's nine?" the man asked. "She looks small."

"She's of age, her name was drawn, and she's untouched." His eyes were fierce, as though he were challenging the noble on each point. To my surprise, the noble bowed his head and turned to his horse. Father knelt before me. "Remember what we taught you."

I nodded, breathless, not daring to say anything in case it came out sounding foolish. Though I knew I was young, as I was constantly reminded, I knew that this was one of those things that only came along in life once. Like a soul-mate or the chance to visit an elderly person. Never knew if they'd be there again in the morning. Others already thought I was a fool, trying to throw knives in tree stumps with boys and slopping through muck in bare feet. No one would think I was a fool for passing up this.

Father rubbed my cheek, and stood up. My sisters had all slipped away, either to watch from a distance, or to tend to chores my mother had set them on. My bet was they were pretending to do chores while watching from a distance. Only Allie came to give me a basket heavy with goods. I wished I could visit to see her married to her blacksmith. A copper betrothal bracelet glinted on her wrist as she helped me upon the pack mule and tied the basket into place. She didn't say farewell, only ruffled my unruly hair, then left. We got along best of the whole family, and I think she was glad to know I was leaving a mere week before she was. She'd made living there tolerable, a peaceful presence among sisters who had formed alliances to exclude me.

"Let us be off, Melody." The noble kept his horse close to the mule, as though afraid I would bolt. As we trudged down the trail, skirting around the closest village, I considered putting my heels into the mule to see how fast he could go. It didn't seem like a good idea, though if it had been my father riding beside me, I would certainly have done it. The most I did was squirm on the mule and pad my seat with a blanket from the pack, which made the mule pause and flick its ears all around, as though asking what I was doing. I patted his neck.

The noble shifted in his saddle to address me squarely. His horse stepped slower, wondering if it should stop, but he nudged it on. "What do you know of dragons?"

What did he mean by that? Did he want a description of a dragon? They were each different. I considered that he was a nobleman, after all, and not likely to know some basic fact, such as for instance, that a male goat was called a buck not a billy. Not that my parents wanted much to do with goats, but I liked them. They were smart. Where was I to start with something more complex like a dragon? "They're animals. Just big, scary ones."

The noble drew his horse up so quickly that the horse flinched and swished his bit with his tongue. "They're demons. Evil. They can act kind and right when you trust them, they'll strike. They'll lie. They'll bribe you. If they like you well enough, they'll turn you into a beast just like them."

He was going to say more, but my glare must have stopped him. Mother always said I had quite the glare, to which my father would always say that he did not envy my future husband. Mother's glares never worked on Father, but my glare seemed to work on the noble. "They're animals. Just like your horse, just like the mule, just like us."

The noble's brow furrowed together. "We are not animals."

"Why not?"

But he had already kicked his horse into a trot, and it took all my effort to stay on the bouncing mule. I simmered angrily, but kept my tongue in check. I didn't want to be sent back to my parents. Imagine the fuss that would cause. Jostling with the mule's unsteady gait, I made a promise to myself that I would only speak when spoken to, and I would give him no reason to even threaten to turn around and take me back home.

My place, wherever it was, was out on this road somewhere. I would find it, even if I had to bite off the tip of my own tongue.

***

Days passed before we reached the valleys of the dragonhaunt, plunging deep into a wild of thorny thickets and ancient trees with twisted limbs reaching for the sunlight. Long ago we had left behind roads kept tidy only for the annual tithes, and now we rode on a narrow path used by deer rather than humans. What few locals there were refused to go beyond the valley where they left their least desirable sheep, a gift to the dragon who lived in the rocks above, where trees would not grow.

I cast my gaze back on the village where we had stopped, much to the amazement of the townsfolk, who had come to see us as though we were travelling entertainers. The noble's man had bought me a cloak, and boots. Had he asked me, I would have declined the gifts. However, it hadn't been a question of if I wanted the items, but had been an order to stand still for sizing. They'd put me in things too large, saying two words, "She'll grow."

Odd that they'd talk of me growing when I saw in their eyes that they weren't sure I would even live. Perhaps they meant to be encouraging. The question in their eyes would have been more alarming, if it weren't for the way adults panicked when they found out we'd gone swimming in a lake, or had mucked about in a bog. They thought everything could kill us. How was a dragon different?

They're demons. Evil. Those words echoed in my head. It was easier to shake the thought while in the sunlight. Father had once said he had too many girls in the house to allow for the world to contain monsters. One night, he had declared that no monster was allowed in his house, ever. From that night on, the youngest sister no longer had night terrors. Now, I wished he had cast that incantation over me specifically.

The best I had now was the nobleman, but his word

wasn't law. The world didn't have to listen to him. Still, he was better than nothing.

When we stood at the opening of the pass leading into the start of the wilderness the noble gazed at it in dejection; I regarded it with curiosity and nervous zeal. Behind us lay fields still barren from winter, but neat and tidy with hedges and rock fences to protect crops which would grow within. Before us loomed great mountains with deep gorges and haunted forests, softened by songbirds and babbling brooks. The harsh drops and steep trails were unlike the meadows shepherds and farmers had domesticated, but I liked it better this way, to think of myself as seeing raw nature as no one had seen her before.

As we scaled our way up a path little more than a large game trail, tangled limbs of trees barred our progress and threw light into a criss-crossed pattern upon the ground. Our voices and footfalls, mine in particular, echoed off great rocks unpadded by the foliage which spring sun promised to provide. Birds of prey, roused by the small game our snapping of twigs startled out of hiding, swooped down upon rabbits and mice from their nests in treetops and cliff faces. Huge trees lay on their sides, their roots clawing at air, some still bedded in the snowy drifts which had taken them down. All in all, it was an adventure of the sort I had dreamed, and my thoughts for tomorrow were cast aside in even the smallest discoveries.

The noble made camp by the road where a clear spring bubbled from the base of the rocks and green-speckled trout darted from the shadow of a rock to the shade of a fallen trunk. Late that night, I huddled against the noble while the wolves howled. He shook his head at me. Once I had tried to tell him that a dragon was no more frightening than any other creature, but the night hid things. In the firelight, eyes gleamed and circled. In the dancing shadows, mysterious things slunk forward and darted back, always at the edge of my vision but never standing before me. Those things were worse, far worse, than any monster I could see.

The man bade me to listen to him. What good would it be if I listened to him, but the monsters did not? I trembled, drawing the cloak tight about my body. I saw white ghosts in the trees. I suddenly wondered if I would have been able to take the sheep onto the mountain that summer.

"Don't be frightened," the man said, stirring the fire and causing sparks to fly. "Dragons don't usually eat the virgins."

"You said they did."

"I was trying to frighten you."

I brushed at the cinders falling on my cloak, wondered if he knew the power of words or if he was more of a fool than I was. Just saying something could bring it into being, didn't he know that? My blood simmered to have such a man as my protector. Nevertheless, I knew that men did not like having their shortcomings laid bare before their eyes. Besides, I might say something untrue and make it true by accident. I glared at him. "And now you don't want me to run. Are you lying again, or do you know what dragons want?"

The man went quiet, and I had my answer.

Spring rain pounded through new leaves. We had only our cloaks, and so we wrapped up in them. The man sang a bar song, then stopped short and looked to me. He went back to arranging wood to dry near the fire. The rain grew harder and harder and the fire died.

I finally went to The Mule and snuggled against his belly, having become friends with the beast of burden despite my best efforts to do the opposite. It never occurred to me to name him anything other than The Mule. We didn't name working animals, and the two sheep dogs Father has were called Black and Mongrel. No sense in getting bonded to things that weren't family, I remembered him saying when I wanted to call an abandoned lamb Midnight. Father had been right about that; the lamb had sickened and died within a fortnight.

I woke while it was still dark, accustomed to getting up to check on lambing ewes. When I remembered that I had no sheep to look after, I rolled over—and saw a ghost in the moonlight.

It was a silvery motion in the fog at first, and my breath caught. They said that those who died lost in the mountains would wander through the ends of their days, looking for the way out, and that they would seek innocent girls and lure them away. My sisters said that if I were to ever see one, I should snuggle tightly in my blanket and hold still. If I were seen, I was to tell them to go away, but to never turn my back on them.

So I didn't run, I didn't move, and I didn't look away as the fog rolled over the blades of grass and embraced me and The Mule in dew drops. My mouth went dry, my fingers cold, and I could hear my heart pound through my veins.

The ghost didn't make a sound between the tree line and when it appeared leaning over The Mule's back. It smelled my hair, hot bursts against my scalp which cooled to a numbing chill.

I tried to whisper "go away" but the words wouldn't come. I slid down The Mule's side and looked upward, into a white face. It was all nostrils at first, its head somewhere between a horse and a deer. Ears pricked towards me and giant eyes blinked, sending droplets off its eyelashes and on my cheeks. It bumped my shoulder with its nose. Its horn was the length of my hand, its spiral nothing more than a faint shadow. I slowly reached up, my hand shaking, and I cupped the coarse hairs of its muzzle in my palm.

The unicorn let out a hot breath, and its eyes drifted shut as its body relaxed.

"You are going to be of great use," came a voice, across the dead fire. "If you can charm the dragon as well."

Those were words worth speaking. Though I feared he would frighten the unicorn away, the beast only twitched an ear at him; then it laid down, and rested its head in my lap until the night gave way to dawn.

CHAPTER 2

After the sun had risen and daylight chased away the shadows of the night, the noble gave me The Mule, my basket, and a blanket. He read from the Bible, and sang with me hymns. Then he bade me farewell, pointing to a deer trail crossing up the side of the mountain.

I began to tremble. For a moment, I doubted. What was I doing, scaling a cliff to meet a monster? Then I remembered the story my father had told me years ago. I remembered the quest we'd made together, a quest to unearth my destiny. There was no place for me there in the village, no trade I could take, and no room in meadows for flocks of my own. Had I been a boy, I might have been taken as an apprentice, but I was no boy. I was a girl, one of many poor girls, and more men were going to war than returning from it.

"Don't be scared," I crooned to The Mule, stroking its neck. "I don't think the dragon will want to eat *you*. Just come along."

There was one path upward through the steep mountain. Pebbles slid beneath my feet, and I leaned against The Mule for support. As I made my way forward, I heard the ruckus of sheep as they emerged from foraging and pressed close. They were old sheep, lame sheep, or in general poor ewes culled from flocks and left to feed the dragon. I wasn't sure what to do with them, but I grabbed at the wool of an older one until she fell in step with The Mule. The other sheep followed us, frightened but without anywhere else to go. Those who strayed would be left to predators on their own; I didn't have time to train them.

When we were almost to the top, The Mule scented something on the wind. His knees locked and he refused to go another step, fear making his eyes bulge, showing white around his brown eyes. Speaking calming words, I removed his tack and let him rest. When he relaxed, I ate from the basket. My sisters had packed me bread and butter and cheese, the second two no doubt being gifts from my mother. I chewed slowly, knowing the market would have paid well for my meal. It made me feel cherished and guilty. They knew how I loved butter, particularly on stuffing. This was probably the best they could do. I shook off reminiscing and thought about the tasks at hand.

I left the animals to graze and continued on my own. Wind blew over my skin, sending goosebumps up my arms. The sun hadn't stopped shining, seeming to watch me as I put one foot before the next, scaling boulders when they came into my path. Every tumble of gravel I mistook for the beat of a dragon's wing.

My fear passed with exhaustion. I scraped my shin when I slipped, then dabbed at the blood with my skirts.

I rested and pouted, but every step took me closer and closer to the dragon's den. And then, I cleared the lip of a ridge, thinking there would be more trail beyond, but I looked up to discover I was there.

Sunlight filled the mouth of the cave, hinting at places where tunnels broke off and went in new directions, the floor polished with use. A trail of smoke drifted out of one tunnel, dissolving into air, marking where the dragon lay. The low, rumbling snore echoed to where I could just barely hear it.

My pants broke the steady exhale of the beast. The rumble stopped, and there came a scraping noise and a flash as light bounced off the dragon's scales as he came into view. He filled the entrance, having to stoop his shoulders and shuffle to move. His wings were pressed tight against his body, but I suspected that if he were to open them, he would be the largest animal I had ever seen. It would be easy to think him evil, or a demon. During the night, he would be a mortifying thing to behold in the sky against the moonlight.

I reminded myself he was no monster, no demon. He was an animal, like me. No greater power had hold of him. He simply was. I mouthed the words, hoping that would be enough to make them real. My hands shook, and so I put down the basket and stepped forward, saying, "My name's Melody."

The dragon stretched its neck toward me, blinking in the light, his scales revealed to be an earthy red. I wondered if they had been brighter when he was younger. The dragon smelled the air, puffs of smoke rushing out of nostrils and forming smoke rings that drifted towards me. The dragon blinked again, pupils forming vertical slits like cat eyes, and the cave groaned as he climbed from his knees to his feet, gaining height. The dragon slid forward, turning his head from one side to the other to get a better look at me. I touched his nose, his scales like leather stretched over rocks. The dragon pulled back.

"Melody," the dragon repeated, his voice like rapids through a narrow mountain river. He blinked at me. I wondered if he knew what to think of me any better than I knew what to think of him.

I wasn't sure what to do now. The stories were different at this point, depending who you asked. Some said that the dragon would ask you questions. Some said the dragon would give you challenges. Still others said the dragon would look into your soul. I held my breath, bit my lip, feeling the loss of my home pressing behind my eyes.

Several rasping breaths passed through his lungs, and still he had made no comment. My hands were trembling. What did the dragon want? Why didn't he speak? I could only shift my feet and draw in the sand. Blisters made the motion painful, but a lifetime of doing without boots made me not want to so much as loosen the laces. The dragon's breath rattled out of its throat and his nose bumped my hip. I staggered back and caught my balance.

"Tell me, Childhe, what is it you seek the most in this life?"

Sweat grew cold on my skin now. What was I to say? No one agreed on the right answer: 'True love', 'contentment', 'three wishes', and so, so many more. One thing agreed was that under no circumstance was one to ask for the dragon's treasure.

"I want to be the virgin sacrifice."

"Why?"

My mouth went dry and I hesitated. It wasn't that I was nervous about the dragon. I didn't have the words to describe the appeal behind the role. "They go places, do things, learn things, meet important people."

"Is it adventure you seek?"

I stared at the great beast, watching me with the stillness of a snake on a cold morning. Was it the adventure? Perhaps on the surface, but I knew he was talking of a desire deeper than that. Why was I here? Why did I leave? Why did I feel I had to leave? Why did the nobleman's words cling to me so much, when all his other comments had fallen like leaves to the ground? At last, I rubbed my fingers together and said, "No. I want to know if the stories are true. I want to know what's wrong, or what's left out. I have to know."

The dragon's breathing stopped and he lifted his head away.

"Knowledge," he said.

With that one word, I wondered if the dragon could give me what I sought—what if he didn't know? Would I make him angry? That was the last thing I had wanted to do. But he merely chuckled, a rasping noise starting in his chest, and his lips parted from his teeth in a smile. He was either pleased, or going to eat me.

Then he drew me against his chest.

"That will take a very long time to gain, Childhe. Your entire lifetime. Do you want to seek out the darkness of the dragon's den and the fineries of the king alike? There is shadow to be found in the brightest place, and light to be found in the deepest dungeons. Is this what you want?"

"I want to know everything," I said. "Everything I can."

"My name is Ragnark," the dragon said. With the flash of a tail, he invited me into his den.

He lit the way with a whisper of magic which sent the crystal veins of the mountainside ablaze the same way fireflies guided the way on a dark night.

I gasped.

"The entire world is magic, Childhe," Ragnark said. "If one will but learn to see it."

When a hare's scream pierced the air, my heart skipped. I tried to sleep that night on the floor of Ragnark's lair, surrounded by the growl of his breathing. A tail twitching in dreams nudged me awake several times. The sand soon felt hard and cold, and I woke while the cave was dark and owls still hunted. Sleep wouldn't return, not with the aches in my body from the hike and the lack of mattress I had slept on my whole life. Exhaustion made me all the more miserable, clouded my thoughts, and cast the world in a gloomy doubt.

The noble's words had burrowed into my skull, growing in strength and melding with other bits of lore and words of caution. In my sleepless state, they all stirred together, forming a sour muddle of confusion and fear. I wanted to know what to do, but nothing in my memory had prepared me for this.

I thought about the dragon. An old parable rang in my head "You become what you are surrounded by". It was meant to keep us away from gypsies and troublemakers. The phrase was often paraded in stories where boys were transformed into asses and girls into sows. I had never believed those stories, not really, but was I willing to risk changing from a girl to a monster? Was it true what the nobleman had said, about the dragons being evil, even when they acted like they weren't? He'd said the dragon would tell me lies. How did I know who was lying unless I heard more than one side of the story? Did the dragons really lie, or was it just what men wanted to believe? I rubbed life back into a shoulder numb from sleeping wrong. What if I found out the truth, but no one else believed me?

Perhaps I should go. I had come and done my duty. The lord of the land cared for his virgins, and I was now one of them, was I not? I stood, thinking that if I were to go, I would need to go now before Ragnark woke. Sand shuffled under my feet, too loud, but the dragon's breathing continued uninterrupted. Then my toes hit his tail and I tripped. I held my breath as his body shifted.

He smacked his lips and yawned. "What is wrong, Childhe?"

I thought quickly. Admitting my true motive would either insult him if he was innocent, or alarm him if he was guilty. What was it my sisters always said?

"I'm cold and hungry."

It was true enough. I was cold and hungry, and far, far more frightened than I thought I'd be. It wasn't fear over the dragon, not entirely. I doubted everything now, when just days before everything had been so certain. It had been predictable and safe, but also trapping. There was risk and danger here. I didn't know which way I preferred my days: safe and stagnant, or daring and full of chances?

A nose bumped my elbow. "Nothing will replace the home you have left behind, and if you were to return, it would not be the same. You have grown since you set foot on the road here. Come lay against me. When you are rested, we will butcher a lamb for you to eat and hang the carcass to smoke and cure."

His words soothed me, gave me back a sense of knowing what was happening. They took away some of the unknown, even as I felt uncertain about killing a lamb on my own. It was a task, to be certain, but I could do it. Slowly, I followed the bend of his neck, stumbled over a foreleg, and then my fingers found his shoulder and then ribs—then the hard scales turned into flesh as soft as my own and very warm. Without further thought, I nestled against his belly.

Drowsiness crept in and out, but sleep wouldn't come again even as aches left my body. I had too many questions, things I wasn't sure if I should ask. When the chill was gone from my flesh and still no sleep had come, I asked, "How do you know to butcher and smoke?"

"I have watched humans a long time, Childhe." Ragnark's voice vibrated through his body and mine. He hesitated, then added, "There are hunters in these woods. Be wary of them. They seek to take what is not theirs, and a woman no matter how young would be a prize just the same as a white stag."

"Why?"

But Ragnark's slow breathing was the only answer to my question. He couldn't have fallen asleep so fast, but when I asked again, he began to snore. I let out an angry sigh and tried harder to find sleep.

When dawn lightened the cave, Ragnark and I went out into the morning air where songbirds chimed in trees and squirrels ran up and down tree trunks. My stomach rumbled. I quieted it with a fistful of bread and cheese from my basket. There wasn't much left, so it was a good thing Ragnark had suggested butchering a sheep.

I lead Ragnark to the sheep flock, careful as I walked down the path, sore as I was from sleeping on the ground and the horse ride. We reached the glen later than I had wanted, and I panted and heaved in exhaustion. The Mule came over to me and rubbed his head on my shoulder. I scratched his ears and his eyes rolled back in pleasure.

Ragnark had been gliding from place to place, being much too large to walk the path himself. He landed on grass and wildflowers next to me. The Mule stepped back, but didn't flee, instead flattening his ears and baring his teeth. Ragnark studied The Mule.

I stepped between them. "Don't eat him. He's mine."

Ragnark snorted and turned his gaze to the sheep who were cornered in briers, turning endless circles around each other like water in an eddy, pushing together tighter and tighter until only the ones on the outside could move.

"Bring one to me," Ragnark said.

I looked over the sheep and picked a sickly lamb,

grabbing it by its front leg and pulling it behind me. I didn't like killing a lamb, but I wasn't strong enough to hold a mature ewe. The lamb struggled against me, but my grip was good and it couldn't jerk free. My fingers went white with the effort, but I wasn't sure I could catch another if this one slipped my grasp. I might lose my nerve at the last second.

"Hold still," Ragnark said when we were close. The lamb froze, too terrified to make a sound, as Ragnark extended his neck so his chin was level with my body. He opened his mouth. Though I'd seen many butcherings before, I was not expecting Ragnark to close his jaws over the lamb's head.

When I realized what was happening, I let go and staggered back, stopping when my heel touched a claw. Ragnark raised his head and swallowed the lamb's head whole. The light drew shadows around his chin, making his beard glisten, still white and without a trace of red.

The body of the lamb, severed at the neck, fell over convulsing and spurting blood onto the newly bloomed cowslips.

"Put its head down hill. Let it bleed out," said Ragnark.

Though he had startled me, the death of the lamb had been much faster than cutting its throat would have been, and it was nice to not have dead eyes staring at me while I grabbed its back legs and pulled them up the hill. I glanced at the rest of the flock, which had not noticed yet that it was missing a member.

"Next time, we should take the lamb farther away from the others. They won't like the blood." Not to mention, the blood might attract other predators to the flock, but I wasn't sure if wolves would risk coming into a dragonhaunt. They seemed to avoid Ragnark's cave.

"Next time we will," Ragnark agreed. "But now, repeat after me. For without death there can be no life, and we must remember the life we have taken and celebrate the life it has given to us."

He began to sing, a low and haunting tone that I did my best to imitate, but it felt strange. Nevertheless, I learned his song as the lamb's body grew quiet then still and stiff.

After the lamb had bled out, I asked Ragnark to bury the blood while I gutted the lamb. Ragnark finished his task with three scrapings of his claws into the earth, then watched me slit the lamb open and empty its cavity. The heart, lungs, and liver were good to eat roasted on a stick over fire, the stomach I thought I could cure to make a water-skin out of, but the treat of everything was the intestines. Washed out—it would have to be very well cleansed to get the scent of sheep milk out of them—and stuffed with herbed bread crumbs and onions the intestines would make umbles. Mother usually made this in the winter as a treat, or so she said, but I suspected it was a filling food when all else was scarce.

My mouth watered at the thought, but to make umbles I would first have to bake some flatbread; Mother had had an iron skillet to hold over the fire, but before they had been able to buy one, she had used thin stones heated over coals. I wondered if there was a bit of flour in the basket that I had missed, and then I wondered if there was a way to get more, or if I would have to find a way to do without. This posed a problem not only for wheat, but everything.

How had other girls survived their time with dragons? And for how long? The stories were scant on those details. Was I expected to do without any items a girl needs? Even forgetting about food, what was I to do when my dress wore through? I knew well enough how to sew, but I didn't have any shears to cut wool off sheep, nor any combs to card the wool. A drop spindle was easy to make, but shears were impossible, and to do everything by myself would take at least a year.

"What troubles you, Childhe?"

I jumped, startled by the dragon's voice. "What am I to do for clothes? I didn't bring any fabric, Mother just sewed with the last of it."

The dragon lifted his head and looked down the direction I had originally come. "There will be offerings for you, marked by bonfire. But you must be cautious and listen well to what I say to you."

"How often are these bonfires?"

"Twice a year, if the villages have abundance, once a year otherwise."

A year. Would I be here that long? Or would I be here for so long that by the time anyone came for me, I had lost myself to the wild and no longer resembled a woman, but rather some sort of vile, growling animal? I looked at Ragnark and couldn't keep a smile off my lips. He wasn't what I would call a vile, growling animal, but then again, I hadn't seen him angry. Would he ever be angry?

I tried hard to reconcile the conflicting opinions in my

mind, my father's view that Ragnark was an animal, my mother's distinct refrain from an opinion, and the noble's thought that dragons were devils. Which one was right? And if they couldn't even agree on this one thing, what else did they not agree upon?

I had no answers, not now. It seemed Ragnark was entirely right about one thing: finding out was going to take a very, very long time. Sighing at myself, I wished I had more patience.

Later that night, I balanced on Ragnark's back to tie a rope around rock outcroppings in his lair. I was hanging the carcass in the smoky haze of the ceiling. In another day or so, I would take the carcass down and we would cut it into strips, then hang the strips to dry.

For tonight, though, Ragnark had started a small cooking fire in the center of his lair. I slid down his rump, landing in sand, and went to check on my searing lamb shoulder. It was burnt on the outside, but inside was moist and hot.

As I ate, I noticed something catching the firelight, something in a pile in the corner of his lair. When my gaze returned to it many times, Ragnark said, "Yes, that is my hoard, Childhe."

I jumped. "I wasn't thinking of taking anything!"

He chuckled, then extended a long claw out to it. When he drew his fist back, a necklace dangled from his smallest claw, blinking in the light.

I took it and lifted it into the air. Ragnark lowered his eyes level to it and nodded.

"What is it?" I asked at last. "It looks like a cross but it's upside down."

"The Hammer of Thor. In days long passed, there were men who came to these villages. They rowed in boats up the rivers and they took all they could carry. I think they would have been particularly fond of you, Childhe, they liked chestnut hair such as yours. As the years went by, they raided less and less and traded more and more. But the people would only trade Godian to Godian. These men were not Godians, but they wanted to trade. So they wore a token to one of their gods that resembles a cross but is not one, so a Godian might mistake them for one of their own."

I frowned. "Isn't silver silver, no matter whose hands it touches?"

"That is indeed a very good question. You may keep the necklace if you wish."

I put it back on his claw. "No, thank you. It is yours. How did you come to get it?"

Ragnark smiled and blew a smoke ring out of his nostrils. "I was watching them one day, and one ship had come ashore without removing the dragon head from the front of their ship, as is their custom. This man who had neglected his duties filled his ship with loot so rich it made even me jealous. I decided I would punish him for his negligence and take his whole ship to my dragonhaunt. Five days later, he found me and gave me that in exchange for my pardon. He never forgot his duties after that."

I looked back into the fire. I didn't know if I should believe him or not. It was a fantastic story, but was it just a story or was it more than that? Was it truth? Father had once said that stories often have more truth than a naked truth by itself, and I wasn't sure if I understood that yet.

A claw tapped on the ground as the dragon watched me. Ragnark said, "If Childhe does not wish to learn, then I will not teach."

"No!" I said, so loud I startled myself. "I...well, they said not to talk about pagans."

"Childhe, you sought me out as your teacher. Do you wish to know what I do?"

I bit my lip and swallowed, then picked between my teeth with my tongue. When I had said I wanted to learn everything, I hadn't thought...I wasn't sure what I was thinking. The fire flickered before me, and I lifted my chin. "If your songs and your herbs are good enough for me to learn, so are your tales. Please teach me them."

Anything he taught that I didn't like I could just ignore. Adults ignored their children often enough, it must be an easy thing to learn to do. I didn't have to tell Ragnark that I was ignoring one thing but not another. He wouldn't know. I just needed him to talk, and I'd learn what I could from it.

Ragnark blinked. First one set of eyelids that went up and down like mine, then a second that went side to side, like a cow's eyes but more obvious. I was only now starting to get used to it. He lowered his head, and told me stories until I fell asleep wondering how long I would be here and tormented with the thoughts of cold winter nights.

CHAPTER 3

My basket rocked on my arm, bursting with willow bark, dandelion, rose-hips, and nettle shoots. My voice warbled through the air, joining in with birds praising the rain our glen had just received. When my tone faltered and broke, I let out a sigh and put my basket down.

"I'll never get this right," I muttered, tying my skirt into a knot at my hip so the hem wouldn't drag through the taller grasses and soak my dress through. Around my waist, I wore the fabric left for me by a smokey bonfire. It had other things, too, a comb and two rag dolls. I took them because I couldn't stand the thought of the dolls abandoned on the rock...that, and I thought I recognized my mother's stitching. Or was I being hopeful?

Red, yellow, and pink leaves shook free from branches and swirled around me. I stopped, and looked back. There had been another bonfire at the start of summer, and Ragnark had warned me to wait until the bonfire died low. He said hunters came to the fire, and I remembered what he had said about hunters taking what wasn't theirs. So I had waited a day, and then gone down.

Someone had left for me a blanket and slippers, and milled wheat in an oilskin bag.

I cast a glance back at the blazing fire, then searched the tree line. No one was there. There were no hunters. Ragnark was trying to frighten me into staying, but why? Stories were all well and good, but some of the things he said confused me. Multiple times he told me that sometime I'd learned during a sermon was wrong. Should I ever try to argue the point, he would stop speaking until I apologized. Either he was wrong or those who taught me were wrong, and I was torn between who to was telling me the truth. It wasn't what I had expected. How could I choose to believe a dragon over the adults who told me often and repeatedly that they loved me and wanted what was the best for me? Ragnark had made no claim to feel even affection for me. And now, I found that by coming here, there was no danger in it at all.

He didn't want me to leave. It was the only reason I could think. I felt foolish for remaining with him all spring and summer. But why did he want me? Was he waiting for me to grow fat so he could eat me? I picked up my basket and straightened my back. If he wanted me round and plump, then feeding me sheep and greenery wasn't going to do the job. But what else could he want?

Something rustled in the bushes. I turned, watching as a man stepped out from behind a tree. He was short and slender, and his skin was pale yet blotted from the sun. His eyes had a wary look about them as he examined me from hair to hip.

"You're the virgin, then? I was expecting someone older." His voice sounded thick and clotted, as though he had hay fever.

Something about his glazed eyes made my stomach knot. "I...I was hoping you could take me back to town. I can't remember the way."

He bared his teeth in a smile. "I can take you. I was planning on taking you all along."

His foot caught a root when he stepped forward and he stumbled.

Heart pounding, I took three steps back, mentally chiding myself for not stepping forward to help him instead. What was wrong with me? Had I been too long in the woods?

But I couldn't force my foot to move towards him. I shied back, feeling like The Mule staring at Ragnark. Still, I wouldn't run away. "Good. Where were you planning on taking me?"

The man's arm shook when he put it on a rock and shoved himself back into a standing position, favoring his leg. He licked his lips and said, "Why, right here. No sense in going anywhere else to do it."

"Do what?"

"You'll see."

There was something wrong with his eyes. It wasn't anything I could name, it was something being shown in them, some emotion I hadn't ever seen before. It chilled me to the bone.

I backed away. "I don't know what you are speaking about. Go away. I don't want you around me."

"Shhh, girl, the dragon has a spell on you. He's keeping you all for himself, can't you see? You don't want to be with him. You want to come with me. I'll take care of you. I can show you the way. I'll hold your hand and keep you close and you won't be able to run or feel afraid because I'll be there, closer than anyone has ever been before. I won't hurt you none. It'll be the two of us, girl, come on, what do you say? Stop your humming, I know you're scared but there's no need." The man smiled, and for a second the song caught in my throat.

He extended a hand, his smile encouraging, the frightening expression in his eyes gone as though it had never been there. Had I been imagining it?

I reached for him, my hand shaking.

In the distance, I heard the rustle of leaves and the beat of Ragnark's wings as he came to my song for help. Confusion and panic hit me at once, a monster coming to the rescue of a maiden. This wasn't how it was meant to happen. Men were meant to be good, and monsters bad. I felt lied-to, tricked. I didn't know by whom.

I yanked back my hand. "No. I can't."

The man lowered his eyes, and when he raised them there was kindness in them. He didn't draw his hand back, not yet. He said, "It's fine. My name is Judas, like from the bible. I've come to save you from the monster."

He reached down the neckline of his tunic and pulled up a silver cross.

I staggered back.

Judas said, "Come now, girl, you know only a true Godian would wear a cross."

"Yes," I said. "But that's not a cross."

"It is! Unless you mean to insult the craftsmanship?"

But I was backing away now, and his smile was faltering. I said, "Judas was a betrayer. And I know that what you're holding isn't a cross. The dragon showed me a necklace like yours. And he told me stories."

Judas put his foot on a rock and his elbow on his knee, chuckling and shaking his head. "And you believe what he says is true? Dragons tell you lies, girl, lies and spells and enchantments. He's turning you into a creature. Come with me, and I'll show you how to be a woman."

"That's no cross."

"Isn't it?" Judas asked, tucking it back into his shirt.

I turned and ran.

Behind me came a curse and the sound of boots snapping twigs and kicking leaves, coming too close, too fast.

I ducked below branches and cut through the forest. There came a grunt and breaking branches.

What little lead I had on him I was losing.

I ran around a rose bush, then hid behind a boulder. I smothered my panting breaths with my hand and squeezed my eyes shut.

Mud sloshed beneath Judas's boots as he went by.

I stayed crouched down until my heart stopped pounding in my ears. Taking a slow breath, I wondered if it was safe to go now. I peered over the rock.

There were young trees poking out of a layer of leaves, and mud speckled around footprints in Judas' trail. The birds had gone quiet.

I straightened up, careful to not make a noise, careful to check my breathing and move as silently as a doe as I turned around—and screamed.

Judas stood behind me, rubbing clean an apple on his tunic. Frozen, I could only gape as he took a knife and cut the apple in half, white flesh weeping clear juice as his blade cut through its skin. He held the parted apple out to me.

"You're pretty with a blush."

I stepped back, feeling my way around the boulder.

Judas sighed. "Don't run again unless you can give a decent chase."

I grabbed a stick.

Judas flicked his knife; it sank straight through the mud at my feet. He held out his hands, half an apple in each palm, inviting me to try fighting him. He warned, "Don't do it unless you can give a decent challenge, girl. I'm a fair man."

I left the knife behind and held the stick out in front of me with both hands. I said, "I don't want to go with you."

"I didn't ask you to."

My brow narrowed. "You said you were taking me somewhere."

That look was back in his eyes again. "No. I said I was taking you."

In two steps he had me by my arms and his face was grinning in mine. How had he moved so fast? What did he want, and what did he mean? What was that smile for?

Then I heard a whisper in the wind, one I knew well, and I ducked. A tail tip rustled my hair, pulling out a few strands, hitting Judas in the face. He held me as he fell, and I tumbled on top of him, jarring my knees, back, and shoulders.

As soon as Judas' hands relaxed, I yanked away,

stumbling, trying to get as far away as I could before he got up again. My back hit Ragnark's leg and I jumped, then laid my hand on his scales.

"He—he's going to get up again," I said.

"He's dead."

"What?" I looked back at Judas. Blood flowed from his nose and his head lay at an odd angle.

I breathed easier. "He—he said he was going to take me, but not take me anywhere. What did he mean by that?"

A long, slow breath poured out of Ragnark's neck. He nuzzled me as I shook. At last, Ragnark nudged me away. "Let us go back to the lair. Do you have the offerings?"

"Yes, but—Ragnark, what did he mean?"

Ragnark's eyes were soft and sad as he looked at me. He said, "You have learned enough for one day. Now is no time for more answers, but instead to take a hot drink by a warm fire and listen to rain trickle down the back of the lair."

CHAPTER 4

I wrapped string about herbs and hung them up on a line, singing a low tune to keep the crystals glowing in the fading sunlight. The den showed heavy sign of my occupation. A gown spread out at the entrance, drying, and against a wall nestled a blanket I'd just mended.

My fourth summer with Ragnark was coming soon. The villagers kept us fed with sheep and me clothed with new fabric. Ragnark taught me his stories, making me repeat them back to him with every word perfect. I learned every plant I saw, their names and seasons and uses. The Mule was my companion when I wanted something besides the dragon, and Ragnark was never tempted to eat him.

I picked up a brush and began to groom Ragnark's scales. They had grown ridged and brittle and had turned dark and dusty. I asked, "How do your shoulders feel?"

"Stiff. I would like more willow."

It was well into spring, but the bushes and trees were still bare like fingers grabbing at my clothes. I had grown wary of humans, stalking the hunters who came to the dragonhaunt, watching the few traders who wandered lonely roads at the edge of Ragnark's territory.

"Do we have any remaining?" Ragnark asked.

"Some," I said, frowning to myself. He knew our inventory, but lately his mind had been slipping the way his body had been.

Of course his mind would be slipping, for all the centuries he had lived and all the things he had seen. He was old, ancient even for a dragon though he had not told me his exact age. He didn't butcher the sheep any longer, and seldom went for a flight.

I pulled down the willow branches, then left him to chew on them while I went to find more. The trail down the mountain seemed smaller than it once was, but I scaled it as though I had wings, and even in the rising moonlight, I was down at The Mule's meadow without so much as a hitch in my breath.

I went to The Mule and scratched the bugs out of his ears, sad that the biters would start to come in swarms once spring began in earnest. Then The Mule dropped off to sleep. I went to the creek in search of willows.

It was some time before I found a patch which had not been harvested. I cut them down and tied them in a bundle over my back, then took a few minutes to stretch in the moonlight. The moon was full and seemed to be at twice its normal size, and the sky was filled with pinpricks of stars, the blackness softened to deep purple and blue. I shivered and started to make my way back.

As I passed over a rock, I peered down into dip below where the creek bent around birch and tall grass. A unicorn doe stood there, licking clean newborn twins as they wobbled on spindly legs. She bumped one with her nose and it fell to its rump and snorted. The other was looking between the wrong set of legs to nurse.

I rubbed my arms to warm them, and watched until both twins were nursing. Last year was the first time I had seen the doe, and she had given birth to a single then. When had I become so accustomed to living in the forest?

A nose bumped my elbow. I looked into the face of the unicorn I had first met. He had grown over the years, too, becoming the size of a small horse and with a foot long horn. I scratched the base of his horn, but he was uneasy, restless. I'd never seen him stand so impatiently before.

Then he looked down at the doe and her twins, and I knew: He was leaving.

I stayed with the unicorn as long as he would let me, stroking his fur and sharing the warmth of his neck. Standing on a ridge, I listened to an owl and I remembered what Ragnark had said last year.

"There comes a time for everything to be born, to live, and to die," he had said, trying to prepare me in case the unicorn had decided to leave last spring.

The beast stepped away from me, and I considered putting my arms around his neck and stopping him.

"There is a time to arrive, a time to stay, a time to go, and a time to let go." The memory of the words kept me seated and I watched as the moon shifted over the unicorn's steps. He made no noise in leaving, as he had made no noise in arriving.

"You have places to see and people to meet, Childhe. Know that everyone around you has the same obligation, and they might not understand it any more than you understand your path."

The unicorn picked his way down a the slope, not disturbing a single pebble, not looking in the direction of the doe and her twins. I watched until his path took him out of sight around a cluster of trees. I knew I should go back up to the den and warm up by Ragnark's belly, but I couldn't.

Then I heard a woman singing.

I followed the unicorn, taking a higher path.

Though I was not as graceful as the unicorn, I knew how to move without breaking sticks or attracting attention. Often I walked upon deer and could watch them for long periods at a time.

The unicorn took a familiar path along the creek, then cut across it. I stood by a birch tree, and then saw a woman braiding grass on the bulge of a hillside. The unicorn paused now and then in the woods, eyeing the woman, twitching his ears this way and that, then advancing again.

She never stopped singing. After a few minutes, I mouthed the words, recognizing it as a song we had sung in church. It seemed like an entirely different life.

Then the unicorn stepped out from the trees. He was tense, picking up his feet high, looking as though he were ready to bolt at the slightest movement. But the woman didn't move, except her fingers. He came closer, his horn lowered at her chest.

She stopped singing, to say something to him.

His body leaned away even as he reached his nose towards her. He was catching her scent. She offered him her braid of grass. His lips took it and he chewed, his chest huffing in and out.

She held out her hand, an invitation.

He stepped forward, his nose lowering to her hand.

Then his whole body froze. My heart skipped a beat.

He lunged forward, diving at her with his horn. She rolled back, taking the blow across her stomach but avoiding impalement. He reared back, seeking to come down on her with his hooves.

An arrow pierced his throat. He staggered back, shook his head, and aimed at her again.

Another arrow hit his chest, in the place where hunters shot deer through the heart. The unicorn swayed. He stumbled. Then he fell over and dark blood spilled over the hill.

I had a hand up to my lips. Living out here had made me mute in times of shock, though I'd never been prone to screaming.

"Anna!" A monk stepped out of a blind. He ran to the woman, his cowl catching the wind and billowing in his face. He wrapped her side with a speed and surety which made me wonder if he had done this often.

I saw now two horses near where the man had come. He brought them over to the girl, put her on one, and the unicorn on the other, then lead his party away.

Wasting no more time, I ran back to the dragon's lair, not caring when I fell twice and once hit my chin on a rock. When I made it back to the den, I was out of breath, sweating, and chilled.

"They killed him! And he stabbed her," I panted when I saw the dragon waiting for me.

Ragnark lifted up his head and stared at me for a very long few seconds, then lifted up a wing. I hobbled beneath it and rested my back against him, breathing so heavy I wasn't sure if I was crying or not.

"Why?" I asked. "Why?"

His voice rumbled over my skin. "There comes a time for everything."

Ragnark rubbed his nose against my shoulder and held his wing tighter against me.

The night had seemed to take an eternity to pass as dreams of blood and men stalked me no matter where I tried to go. Sleep had come sometime in the morning, and I deliberately did not ponder on the hunt which I had seen. My eyes were sore and my chest felt tight, but more than anything else, I felt heavy. I wanted to forget everything from last night, but I could not.

It was nearly midday when I woke to an empty lair. I didn't want to be alone, where thoughts and dreams haunted me. I found Ragnark at the mouth of the cave stretched out in the sun. I watched him flex his wings. "Are you planning a flight today?"

"Yes. I would like to go down to the valley where the snow drops are blooming. Grab your basket."

It had been some time since he had told me to get that.

I hurried to toss what few items I had left into the basket, then came to sit in his claw, resisting the urge to ask. Ragnark did not like me to ask why he took his time standing, nor why his scales had one by one become brittle and filled with ridges. I found myself looking after him with greater and greater concern.

"Hold tight," Ragnark said.

"Of course," I replied, a bit too harshly, but it was because he had made me worried. Never before had he told me to hold on.

One final time, we launched off the small cliff and soared over the treetops, hair and wing-tips tousling in the wind, following the creek winking through bare trees. All too soon, we landed, and the dragon heaved in exhaustion.

For two days I cared for him, finding the herbs he had taught me to make him better. A low rumble came from his chest when I began the broth. "Childhe," he said, his tone sympathetic, "I am dying, little one."

"Dragons don't die." Even when I said it, I knew they did. It took a sorcerer and a man good with a sword, one to break the spells, one to break the soft plate under the dragon's chin. When a dragon's den lay empty, young dragons laid claim to it. Young dragons ate more, sought mates, and were more likely to destroy towns. This was why the King gave the dragons virgins. Fewer people died.

"I have something for you."

At first, I didn't respond to him. But I couldn't deny him for long. I stretched out my hand at his bidding, and looked up to see Ragnark working his fang free with his claw. His forked tongue darted over the deep cavity left behind, licking at the blood.

Ragnark spoke a few words, and the tooth began to shrink. It became smaller and smaller until it slipped out of his claws. I caught it on the way to the ground and studied it. It was now the size of a bear claw. He told me to keep it, so I tied it in string and put it around my neck.

I used my blanket to stop the bleeding at his gum line, and I tried to not cry.

He taught me a song. The notes strained my throat, but he made me practice it over and over again. I knew a good variety of dragon songs now, and I swore I would never forget them.

When I tired, I pressed my head over his heart, listening to it as it slowed and skipped, then took two beats as though to catch up.

"Listen," Ragnark whispered, "until I turn cold, little one. No magic may ever fool you. This is the final gift I give to my friend."

I listened, but all I heard was his heart slow and slow, and his breath rattle. Then his heart gave one final push and fell quiet. Then the air seeped from his lungs and the echo of his last pulse faded away until all I heard was the sea rushing in my own ears.

When I leaned back from the cold body, the scales began to change color, going from muddy red to earth brown, one scale softening into the other. Vines, moss, and grass reached for him, transforming the body of the dragon into yet another hill, just a bulge in the ground exactly like any other.

No one would know this was Ragnark. Unwilling to do anything else and uncertain if the man would even pass by, I held vigil in the valley until the noble came once again.

CHAPTER 5

The noble rode to the same place where we had made camp, and I watched as he set up camp again, unsaddling his horse and brushing him until his coat shone under the fading sunset. I watched as he struggled to light wood dampened by rain.

I looked up the mountain again and knew that the cave would be hollow without the dragon waiting for me. Sometime in the last few days, The Mule had abandoned the sheep flock and joined me, and now The Mule turned his ears to the noble and let out a slow snort. I rubbed his ears.

The noble threw down his sticks and huffed off to his packs, finding hard bread and cheese. The Mule cropped grass, wandering slowly towards his horse. I stepped forward, too, approaching the man from behind, watching him warily. He had done me no harm as a child, but would he recognize me now? As the lord's man, his duty was to keep me safe, but still I wondered if I could trust him.

With a pocketful of dry moss and the shell of a honeycomb, I soon had a small fire started. I was feeding it sticks the thickness of my fingers when the noble turned around. He jumped and pounced on his sword laying on his cloak in the grass.

"Who are you?" he demanded, sword at a ready stance. Seeing that I was unarmed, he might have felt silly, but if he did then he showed no sign of it. What harm could a bladeless woman pose to one like himself, I wondered.

I raised my eyes to his, saw the worry and the fear in them, and smiled. Whatever fear he had of me, it wasn't going to go away until I let him know who I was. Flames took hold of the end of a stick, so I rearranged it to be in the center of the fire. "I told you sheep are better to eat."

Confusion marred the noble's brow, and his jaw gaped open. His sword tipped downward. "Melody?"

I nodded.

He sat down heavily on a rock in front of me, his face pale and his sword hanging awkwardly in his grasp. "What happened? Did he let you go?"

I showed him Ragnark's tooth, but before I could explain, I started to weep. The noble stood and dropped his cloak over my shoulders. He studied the landscape, then walked in the direction of Ragnark's mound.

I was too fatigued and lost to feel embarrassed by my outburst. Had it been anyone else, though, I wasn't sure if I would have felt comfortable baring my grief. Or, for that matter, if anyone else would have understood. Typically people greeted the death of a dragon as a mixed blessing and nothing more. They wouldn't have thought to shed a tear for one. The noble had not admonished me, though. Perhaps his experience with dragons gave him broader understanding of the emotions they aroused.

While it was me and The Mule by the fire, I briefly wondered what would happen to me. It felt wrong to try to go back to my parents now. I knew too much, and yet I knew nothing. In my time, I had learned two truths: The human truth and the dragon truth. Sometimes they were one and the same. Sometimes they were much, much different. What I hadn't found, yet, was the only truth that really mattered: My truth. What I decided I wanted to believe and put my faith and trust in. Sometimes I thought I knew, and other times...other times I wondered if I was wandering circles in an endless forest at night. It wasn't a comforting thought, but I reasoned that I would have to keep trying to push forward. Where I found myself was where I found myself. I had a direction, but not a destination. Perhaps that was for the best. Perhaps that was disaster. One way or another, I would find out.

It was an hour later that he returned. He put food in my hands and commanded me to eat, then said, "We leave at first light."

Having another person with me was a comfort. Different from my dragon companion, but more talkative than The Mule. As well, the noble knew how to cook, and I cherished having a meal that I didn't have to prepare myself, even if it didn't taste as seasoned as I'd make. The fire died low, and I accepted a new blanket. It was the first night since Ragnark died that I slept well.

The noble bought me a horse and new clothes, and I rode with him for three weeks on a circuitous trek which took us to settlements even smaller than my old village. The road was a long and weary one, but I did not complain. We slept in cottages off the road, ones stocked by locals for the king's men to stay in, and at times we camped without shelter. Still other times we ventured into an inn, under the guise that he was my father. Cooking and clean up duties alternated night to night.

He never offered his name, and once I heard whisper that he didn't have one. His father had betrayed the king, so the king had executed the traitor, and stripped the family of title, name, lands, and wealth of any kind. The king had given my escort the ability to serve him instead of begging on the streets, but had refused to give him a name. When we were out of range of other people's hearing, I started to call the man Noble. I wasn't very creative in my naming, but I thought Noble was a fitting description of his temper. He never objected, though he did ask if I was likely to number my children instead of naming them. If it were a task up solely to me, that might very well happen.

We ventured on roads maintained by many villages to promote trade lined with trees with the lowest branches trimmed so they wouldn't block the road after a storm, and on roads which started off as muddy tracks for carts which disappeared into trails marked by a flat spot in the grass and rocks to denote a place to turn.

When the three weeks had ended, Noble bade me to dismount at the stoop of a mountainside cottage which wore its roof as low as a cowl. A garden was starting of its own accord from last year's seed, but a man in a robe tore up the earth with a hoe, flinging mud and seedlings into the air. He stopped when he saw us.

He was a lean man, a man hardened by snows and blistering sun, and in his eyes I saw that he was far from pleased to see me. In an instant, that look was gone and he turned his gaze to Noble. I frowned to see a variety of clay bowls, each with vegetable seeds in the bottom.

"It will frost late this year," I said, "all you plant now will be frostbitten and die. You'd best wait a week or two longer."

The man only stared at me, even as Noble gaped at me as though I had grown scales. Noble shook his head and said, "This is Melody, the girl who lived with the dragon." A pause, then the man in the robe twitched a frown. Noble added, "He's dead now."

"He was old," the man in the robe said. He looked me over with the same scowl he gave the garden as he decided which plants to weed out. "Three years, yes? Yes. It will take longer than that to erase the lies he has whispered into your ears, assuming you aren't beyond the point of saving. Come, come. My name is Brother Jacob. Brother Adams has food for you both inside."

It sounded less like an invitation and more like a courtesy unwillingly offered. I thought about storming off into the woods, insulted by both his implication that I was tainted and that Ragnark had taught me lies. Perhaps *some* of the things he said were lies, but not all. I couldn't be certain that this Brother Jacob would teach anything more truthful than what Ragnark had. Whoever this Brother Jacob was, I did not like him at all. Nevertheless, I picked up my basket and went into the cottage.

Inside, the cottage resembled the house I had left at the farm, but more cluttered. In a single room, there were four beds, three of them made up nicely while the fourth seemed to serve as a piling ground for laundry, books, and half-finished stitching projects. I suspected that bed was mine, and that they had not been expecting me.

Against one side of the wall, two desks made of legs and a slanted top nestled next to a longbow and arrows in the process of having their fletching mended. In the middle of the house was a strong fire, perhaps a bit too smoky, but when I looked into the rafters, I saw fresh fish hanging by their gills. Someone brought a table out from its resting place behind a bed and set it up down the center of the beds, so we sat down on the mattress to eat at the table.

Noble held non-stop banter with the brothers, leaving me to pick at a watery pottage of oatmeal colored with a dab of milk. Across from me, a girl dressed in a long sleeve gown of undyed greyish wool tried to coax me into conversation, but I didn't know what to say. What if I said something to insult her, or worse, to appear foolish? Better to hold my tongue and say nothing at all.

After the way Ragnark had been taken from me, I was hesitant to make friends with a new person. Particularly if she was a sacrifice like me, and could be dead by Easter of next year. As she continued to chat and refused to accept my mute replies, I found I was starting to like her despite myself.

The next day, Brigid laughed at me.

"You sing so funny! It's like you're growling," Brigid said, tossing brown locks over her shoulder, wobbling a little as she tried to balance on a rotting log. All night and early morning she had talked at me, getting no more than one-word answers, until she hit upon the idea for us to go on a walk. The brothers had instantly agreed. I think they wanted to talk about me in private, but then again, the whole world wasn't centered around me.

I tried not to be insulted by Brigid's giggles. I walked out on a tree branch, stepping lightly as the branch grew narrower and more brittle.

"Be careful," Brigid called, worried.

I stopped and looked at her. She might have been older than me, or possibly younger. Brigid's age was not easy to tell; she had the round face of eternal youth and the occasional bout of wisdom well beyond her years. Her eyes were nothing special—most of the time. Every now and then, though, they narrowed and it seemed she could look into my mind and tell what I was thinking.

"How long have you been a virgin?" I asked. She seemed older than I was, if not by much, and I was curious about this sister of sorts that life had given me.

She gazed at me through lowered lashes and said, "All my life."

I snorted. Like a dragon. Like Ragnark. Then I remembered the red dragon, and I jumped down to the grass. The limb cracked behind me, but I didn't pay any heed to it, instead I eased into a long stride that left Brigid jogging. If I stayed there, she would be as a sister to me. I'd already given Allie up for this life. I'd already lost my mentor. I wasn't willing to bond with then lose yet another friend. When I met the brothers, it was different: I didn't like them, so losing them wouldn't have caused me grief. But this girl...this was different.

"Wait up," she called.

I didn't. I didn't want anything to do with Brother Adams or Brother Jacob and particularly not Brigid. I wanted to run into the bent tangles around us, dive into the deep shadows and never emerge again. As I ducked below a branch, I knew I wouldn't have to come back. I knew the edible plants, how to make shelters, and how to hunt and cook.

The woods had become heavy with dew and ferns, the trees a crow's nest of ensnaring fingers, and the only light came from behind me. A voice drifted to me from that hole. "Wait! Melody! I didn't mean it, I was teasing, please come back."

I knew she had been teasing. That didn't mean I'd liked it, but neither was I surprised. Before she'd done that, I had almost forgotten myself around her, almost let her make friends with me. I had always been teased. Teased for lying in the sun, teased for sitting and listening to anyone willing to spin a tale, teased for learning how to do boy things.

The only one I'd felt at home with was Ragnark, and he had died. I knew now he had called for a virgin so he wouldn't have to die alone. Tears stung my eyes again, and I rubbed at them angrily. None of that. He'd taught me valuable things. It was a fair trade. That didn't make the pang in my chest lessen any, though.

"Please? I promise we'll go looking for unicorns now." Brigid's voice shook. There came a rustle and a smothered scream. I suspected it was the badger I had seen on the way down here. How could that girl be so clueless? She asked, "Melody?"

Before me there was a small clearing in the trees, just right for me to stretch out in and bask in the light coming through the leaves. The grass was bright green, and yellow flowers dotted the rocks. Behind me was a cottage with two grumpy monks in it devoting all their love onto books.

Brother Adams said he would teach me to read them. I didn't know what that meant at first, but now I realized that with the ability to read them, I could learn anything that was recorded. If I continued into the wood, I wouldn't learn anything new. It would all be the same. Brigid's form still blocked out most of the sun, and I could tell she was too terrified to step in.

If I went back, the Brothers would teach me to read, and maybe more.

One way was freedom.

The other was servitude.

I had gone to the dragon looking for that freedom. I wanted to be out from under my parents' watchful eyes. I wanted to shed the reputation of my elder sisters and shake off the burden of the younger girls.

And so I had. But now it was traded for one girl and two adoptive fathers. I had told Ragnark that I wanted to learn everything there was to learn. He had warned me it would be a lifetime pursuit. Had I been too quick to agree?

I closed my eyes and thought.

Reading and writing was rare, very rare. I would never

have the money to pay for such schooling...unless I returned to a dragon and traded him for some of his treasure. Even so, people would wonder where I had gotten the money. I would be labelled a thief or returned to the Brothers.

A wren sang above me, hopping down from branch to branch to better see me. This was the only chance I would ever get to learn the ways of parchment and ink. Was that what I wanted?

I whistled a song. The wren turned his head and sang back to me.

I circled through the trees, careful to step on stones so I wouldn't accidentally break a stick. I startled Brigid when I said, "Let us go find a unicorn, then."

She threw her arms around me in a hug. I swayed under her weight and patted her back, uncertain about what to do. Brigid pulled back and gave me a beaming smile.

"This way," she said and jaunted off towards the road.

The smile faded from my lips when I thought about the cold cottage with the bland oat pottage I would have to return to. I looked longingly after the wild woods, and I left them behind.

Smoke rose out of the chimney when we came back to the cottage. Brigid took a deep breath of air and declared, "Food!"

It wasn't anything like the roasted meat I'd eaten with Ragnark, and I said so.

Brigid shot me a look to shush me, and said, "Don't you say that in front of the Brothers. They'll make you do penance in the dark room. Too much meat makes men quick to anger. Certainly you ate only plant matter on Wednesdays?"

"Of course," I lied. In truth, I hadn't a clue what day of the week it was, and my parents had never stressed the meatless days because they would always trade any meat from the sheep for vegetables from the neighbors.

"Even the king doesn't eat meat on Wednesdays," Brigid said with a confident smile. She nudged the door open, and the two monks nodded to us by way of greeting.

"What did you do today?" asked Brother Adams as Brigid trotted up to the fire, rubbing her hands together and sniffing the pottage with a grin.

"I showed her snow drops and told her that they come up where unicorns have been. And the clear springs, but she knew that one already, everyone knows that one, and I showed her how to kneel down, but nothing came to us."

Brother Jacob said, "I would think not. She's new. It will take them a few weeks to grow accustomed to her scent."

"And I taught her new hymns!" Brigid shot me a broad grin. "We're still working on her singing voice, but she's better."

I sat down on a bed and drew the blanket around my legs, feeling so chilled in this cottage instead of warm, curled against a dragon's belly in the sun.

Brother Jacob frowned at this. "What does she sound like?"

Brigid went a little pale. She stammered, "Can't hold a note is all."

I wondered what they would do if I gave an example of how I 'couldn't hold a note', but decided that my life was going to be miserable enough without doing penance in this fabled dark room. Who knew what they would do to make me forget? When they had asked me what it was that Ragnark had taught me, I had said nothing, but that had been out of pain over his death. From Brigid's reaction, I would be smart to never say anything of my dragon education.

Brother Jacob didn't look like he believed Brigid. He asked me, "Does she speak the truth?"

Frightened eyes turned toward me, but I didn't meet them. That would be too obvious. I said, "When I lived alone, I thought I sounded fine."

Brigid looked relieved. Brother Jacob slopped food into bowls and passed them around. When everyone had a bowl and a spoon, Brother Adams said, "Melody, would you say the meal prayer?"

My heart pounded and my mouth went dry. I had no idea what to say, and they were expecting a prayer. What had they said when they first brought me here? I couldn't remember.

I hadn't so much as prayed when I was living with the dragon, but that was obviously not going to be a good answer. Instead, I lowered my gaze and softly muttered something my mother used to say over the squabbling of my sisters.

Brother Adams leaned forward with his ear leading the way, trying to catch the words I intentionally slurred. Then I ran out of sounds to make and glanced at Brigid, who mouthed "Amen". I declared the final word just as softly as the rest of the performance, "Amen."

"Amen," came the chorus.

Brother Jacob said, "We are going to have to teach Melody to not be so shy."

I raised the quiet question to Brigid, who nodded. She would teach me the prayers.

After dinner was a prolonged reading from the books. Brigid sat next to me with a book, and I spent that entire evening studying the illuminated letters on each page, admiring the illustrations. At the sight of an "S" with the head of a dog, I couldn't help but to reach forward and stroke its forehead.

Brigid said, "Brother Jacob does those."

Surprised, I looked at the man with the hard face who said very little. Brigid nodded, "They say the unicorn blood gives him special talents, but he says its a gift from God, and that alone."

"Why do we hunt unicorn?" I asked.

Brigid raised her brow in surprise. "For the communion."

"I heard some villages take wine and bread."

"They do," said Brother Adams, cutting into the conversation. He explained, "There is no shame in such a humble display, but the unicorn only sacrifices itself for the purest churches as represented in people like us. We eat of his flesh and drink of his blood, and his soul rises again in the forest. When we see the risen unicorn, then we may make use of his hide, hooves, and horn in a manner befitting the church."

It didn't make sense to me, but then again, I had never understood communion. I considered asking further, but decided that it might launch us into another discussion, and my head ached as it was. I felt suffocated by the presence of all these people and trapped in a small house. So I asked no more questions, and I bluffed my way through the rest of the lessons.

The next day, we woke Brigid early and went to church to make my appointment as a virgin sacrifice official.

CHAPTER 6

I'd been to service many times, though obviously not since I had been living with Ragnark. After we descended a steep trail and found our way down the one true street of the village, we arrived at a building of lumber frame and adobe coating with tall windows made of smaller sections held together with lead. It was far more impressive than the other church I had attended, one sharing a wall with the inn. These communities did the best they could do, as simple as that.

Inside, the building had a high ceiling, even though I had expected it to have two floors and a loft. It seemed a waste of space, but I was wise enough now to realize that it wasn't a waste, it was a display. That was why there was moulding around the pillars, and that was painted blue and yellow, also why the candle holders were made of silver. At the far end of the church was a small door disguised behind a scarlet drape; I wouldn't have noticed it, except it opened to let a short, bald man in black robes into the church. When he saw us, his face was soon lost to a great smile. He opened his arms out, as though he were going to embrace all four of us at once. I hung back while Brother Adams slapped his shoulder.

"You're here before the choir! When you brought Brigid, you could hardly make it through the door." The man in black then turned to Brigid and gave her a hug, which she returned.

"Brother Frances," Brigid said, her cheeks starting to turn pink. "We weren't that late."

I glanced around us, at all the open room. What did he mean they could hardly get through the door? How many people came to services? My musings were disrupted when Brother Jacob stepped to one side. "This is Melody."

Brother Frances came to greet me, but I glanced at his arms and tried to look as though I didn't want to be touched. He instead clapped a hand on Brother Jacob's back, to which Brother Jacobs twitched a frown. Brother Frances didn't notice. He was looking at me. "From where do you hail, Melody?"

Had no one told him about Ragnark? I met Brother Jacob's eyes, and Brother Frances said, "Yes, I know about the dragon, dear child. I mean, from before then? Who were your parents, and what did they do?"

Child. It was much too close to childhe. I needed to put that as far behind me as I could. Still, I thought that the brothers would want me to tolerate this Frances as much as possible. "They raised sheep."

"Yes, but what were their names, child? What is your surname?"

I stared at him as blankly as I could, trying to smother the anger at the word child. What did he want with their names, besides? "I called them Mother and Father."

Brother Frances's face-eating smile faded. He looked to Brother Jacob, and catching his glare, he let the man go. "At least the name of the town, then? I can't very well introduce her as Melody of the Dragons, can I?"

"Weaverham was the closest civilization with a recognizable name," Brother Jacob said. "Not precisely where she's from, but it'll satisfy curiosity."

Brother Frances nodded, then waved as several people entered the church and headed to a chest, where they took out black robes similar to the one Brother Frances wore, but much shorter. When they thought I wasn't watching, or had my back turned, they talked about me. I had better hearing than they thought I did. They were curious, like Brother Jacob had indicated. My stomach clenched and I fought down the urge to hide.

Brother Frances's smile faded entirely, and he spoke to Brother Jacob as though I weren't standing right in front of him. "Does the child speak at all?"

"Don't call me child," I snapped, angry at hearing the term of endearment come from a short, bald man. When his eyes widened and Brother Jacob looked to the floor and rubbed his brow, I added, "It's what the Dark One called me."

Using that term had the desired effect, for instantly Brother Frances and the choir people gasped in surprise, and Brother Frances took hold of my hands in apology. "Oh, dear! I truly did not mean to cause distress. Surely it must have caused distressed. Who wouldn't be struck mute upon being reminded of such trials?"

I accepted his apology in soft tones. Brother Jacob caught my eye and raised a brow, knowing me too well to think I was 'distressed' over the dragon. I tried to give him a smile, and his lips softened as he shook his head once. It was as though he actually approved of my manipulating Brother Frances.

Many minutes later, after the brothers had found and put on identical crimson robes and Brigid had helped me into a white gown which was too tight in the shoulders, I heard the choir and Brother Frances alike whispering to newcomers about the alarming 'distress' I'd already had today. They were going to think me weak and silly. I wondered what I could do to put them right.

"Hold your tongue, Melody," warned Brother Jacob. Either he knew me better than I thought he did, or my frustration was showing.

"They'll think I'm a foolish girl."

"They'll know better than to speak of Dark Ones around you. Best not to let you get talking about dragons and Ragnark."

Brother Jacob's jaw was set, and his eyes were watching as the room continued to fill. It was three-quarters of the way there now. I suspected services would start soon; there didn't seem to be much space left. Still, I wondered. "Why not?"

He sighed, then leaned down to my ear to whisper. "You were with him a long time. You struck a deal with him, you had to have, otherwise one of you would have been dead within a year. I would rather that no one else comes to this realization."

Deal with a Devil. Witchcraft. Words I'd heard before, and paid little true attention to. I never thought it would be said in connection with me, but now I wondered.

Similar rumors had been spread with less truth in them. The thought made me shiver, and I examined rafters carved with various faces mocking those they guarded. What if I had made a deal with something evil? But that couldn't be. I refused to believe it. And it was that mute refusal that had me wondering if I was any better than those who stood on a platform and burned over a bonfire. Brother Jacob was right: no one else should know.

Brother Frances motioned us to stand against the front of the church, so we were facing the congregation. Behind us was a wall of human bodies dressed in short, black robes. Brother Adams and Brigid stood to Brother Frances's other side, and I wondered for an instant if I had chosen Brother Jacob or if he had chosen me. Soon, I didn't care.

People crowded in so thick that they had to cross arms to keep from touching another person on the hips or butt. They turned the air humid and sour with too much breathing, making the room hot and eerily quiet. The windows could not open, so there was no draft in the room, nothing but dusty scents from hangings directly overhead. Burning sandalwood incense, too hot, and too close for comfort. By the time Brother Frances addressed the congregation, my head was already spinning.

Brother Jacob's cardinal red cloak brushed my hand, the only thing keeping my feet in place. There were so many faces. One man in particular was staring, nothing sinister, just unnerving. Reminding me of Judas. A boy sang into my ear, higher than the pitch of a screeching bird, leading the walls of bodies into an incantation as frightening as the silence which had preceded the unicorn. I was surrounded on all sides, particularly when those before me sang, a random ruckus of off-tones and missed words.

Now it wasn't just the shoulders of the gown which were too tight. It was the chest, too. I couldn't breathe. The walls wobbled, as though they would come crashing down. I told myself that those who leaned against the walls couldn't push them inwards. They'd fall outwards. Then the roof would come down. A face carved on the end of a nearby rafter jabbed its tongue out at me, mocking. Was this what it felt like when the church rejected you? Was I not meant to be here?

That man was staring at me still. It was obvious; he was a head taller than everyone else, towering over even Brother Jacob. I tried to ignore him, and focus on the words Brother Frances was saying. I'd already missed some of them.

"We must guard Melody, protect her from evil and a tainting word. White cloth, once stained, may never again be unsoiled, so watch her well, and lead her not into temptation and foulness, but keep her high off the muck."

All around me, heads were bowed or nodding, a few stealing glances at me as though I were a relic on display. Some women smirked, as though they knew the truth, they knew that Ragnark had taught me things I should not have. They knew I was undeserving. The heat in the room was only growing as the sun came though the windows and shone directly on me. I started sweating.

Brother Frances was oblivious to the way his flock was receiving me, his head turned up to the windows, staring into the light as though it weren't making tears stream down his face. "Let her know only peace and love and a strong heart, so she may face the darkness stemming from our own sins."

Who told him what had happened in that cave with Ragnark? The dress tightened around my chest, making my breaths come quicker and more shallow. Too many people breathing. They were taking the freshness away, leaving it like bad air in a mine. I bunched my dress in my fist. I wouldn't be frightened into not learning. They couldn't stop me. Hot and cold bursts warred in my body.

Brother Frances raised his voice. It boomed from him and bounced off the back wall of the church, startling me to think that such loud words could come out of a man so small. "Every time you look upon her, be shamed. Be shamed, since it is your dirty secrets that is the reason our angels upon the earth must face impurity in our stead. These two girls, Brigid and Melody, they are stronger than we are, and more powerful, not inclined to the weakness I see in all your hearts. It is our duty to keep them safe and pure. Be cautious in what you speak to them, for an offhanded comment may be all it takes to ruin a white cloth forever."

The crowd shrunk back, and many people shifted or murmured to one another, yet didn't seem too surprised. It was as though they were accustomed to his fire and brimstone voice. I, however, was not. What did he mean it was their duty? Did he mean that they wouldn't let me leave? What if they were to learn that I had been stained, tainted, and by a dragon at that? What if they learned about Judas? Sweat ran down my back, making the dress cling to my skin. Was I staining it?

Brother Frances bowed his head and raised his hands, and everyone in front of me did the same. I wondered if I was supposed to as well, but Brother Jacob met my gaze and gave me a half-smile. He didn't raise his hands, and neither did Brigid or Brother Adams. Whispered prayers hummed through the air, and someone sniffed as though they were crying. My stomach twisted and I fought back the thought that they would find out about me and those hands would turn against me.

"Now, join with me in a song of prayer and thanks for this miraculous addition to our great and glorious family." Brother Frances's cheery voice caught me off-guard, but the congregation once again seemed used to it. They stretched necks and shifted, as though preparing to leave. Once again Brother Frances boomed, "Sing praises for Melody, the newest bride of the church!"

Bride of the church. Bride. When did I get married? Who had made that choice in my stead? That man, the tall one with bulging eyes and wood shavings on his tunic, was grinning at me as though he had known about it all along. My stomach was churning, but I couldn't feel it anymore, it was as though the sensations were happening to someone else and I was watching these events unfold for someone else. But it was me! It had to be me. Had I trespassed by coming into the church? Was I going to die? Behind me, the choir stepped forward, crowding me towards the leering man.

When I balked, black robes swirled around me, advancing upon the congregation. Soon I couldn't see the visitors anymore. Everything all around me was black silk rustling and catching the light, like a great shadow coming out of nothing and pushing me around. I couldn't breathe. The room spun. I had to get out. Black, sea of black. Couldn't tell myself that these were people, not a monsters. I had to get out. Pushed one way, then another. Out, where was the way out? Suddenly the black sea let up, and I shrank away from it.

My back touched the wall. The choir was mingling with the common folk, now, and I vaguely recalled that happening a time or two in our much smaller church. It was probably expected for me to join them, but there wasn't enough air in here. I needed out, before they came back and crushed me again. I remembered the door which had been open when we first came in. I found it and slipped through, feeling lost without the red cloak of Brother Jacob.

On the other side of the door was Brother Frances's home, or at least I suspected it was his. The bed, tucked in place in the corner with a blanket draping around it, looked like it was made by the same person who had made the beds in the Brothers' cottage. The ceiling was tall, a match to the church, but it was completely clear of smoke. In fact, there was no place for a fire in this one-room home. There was a table and a few clay items on a shelf, no decorations on anything. I suspected that our cottage would look similar except for the touches that Brigid and I left everywhere. Finally my breathing started to come to me again, but I was still dizzy.

Brother Jacob entered, coming to a stop by my elbow, his face flushed and his hairline damp. He took one look at me, then reached for a pitcher, poured water into a cup, and gave it to me. He made another one for himself. "Drink it slowly."

Once my lips touched the water, warm and dusty as though it had been sitting out for the morning, I couldn't stop from taking several gulps. "It's too hot in there."

Brother Jacob took the cup away, but it was too late. Already I was feeling the twists in my stomach come more violently. He frowned. "There's a meal after. It'll be cooler. It's by the river. They'll want to see you there."

My chest constricted and the room spun floor to ceiling. As my stomach gave a final heave, I found an empty pot and vomited into it. When I was done, Brother Jacob's rubbed the spot between my shoulder blades, as my mother had done before him. I cleaned up, shaking from hands to knees. When I thought of all those people, of the sea of pressing bodies, my stomach lurched again. "I can't do it. All those people."

When I raised my gaze to his, I saw the set of his lips, and knew he was going to fight me. He said, "So this is your fear? You'd best face it."

"I don't want to." What I felt now wasn't fear, but anger, hot and pulsing through my shuddering limbs. "You can't make me. I won't do it."

He raised a hand. "Then I won't, but you should."

Brother Jacob clacked the rim of the pitcher to the cup, and offered it again. I drank more slowly this time, but was glad that someone had drawn cool, fresh water from the well. He watched me for a minute. "Perhaps it is best that you remain crowd-shy."

"What do you mean by that?"

"I mean to say that the best way to keep a white cloth

clean is to keep it away from all but the most careful of people."

My cheeks heated and I put down the cup. "I'm a person, Brother, not a cloth."

"So long as they only ever see you, all you'll be to them is a cloth. Something to look at and use and care-for. If you want to be a person, you need to show that to them."

I bit my lip and let out a slow sigh, not knowing if he was right or not. But I knew that unless I talked to him, the tall man with bulging eyes would forever be the creepy person who stared at me. I knew nothing else about him, and likewise he knew nothing else about me. To think of it that way made it a comfort, actually. The shaking in my limbs faded as the slow sips of water restored me. "I've had enough for one day. I'm not hungry."

"We can't avoid church, Melody."

Brother Jacob answered a light rap on the side door, and a tiny woman in her prime entered with a now-clean pot. It was the one I'd been sick in. She looked me head to toe and said, "Twas the heat that did you in, wasn't it? You look better now. I'm the healer here."

The woman gave me an idea.

"Can we come on the days that aren't so hot?" What I really wanted to ask was to come on the days when there weren't as many people, but it was impossible to predict the size of a crowd in advance.

Before Brother Jacob could answer, the healer said, "I insist upon it. Brother Frances will be in a fit over it, seeing how the snows seal up your road in the winter, but he'll listen to me."

"As you'll have it," Brother Jacob said, but I couldn't get over the resigned disappointment in his voice.

CHAPTER 7

By the time spring came, I was sneaking books to my mattress and reading by candlelight, and Brother Jacob saw. I had learned to sing hymns the way Brigid did all through the summer, autumn, and winter. She taught me to read, too, first the letters, then sentences. Our visits to the church weren't nearly as traumatic as the first time, but neither had the building been so full as on that day. We attended services infrequently enough that I rarely had to worry.

Days ago, one of the villagers brought a chair to the house and Brother Jacob put it by the fire.

"Come read where the light is better," Brother Jacob ordered.

I hesitated, then did so, sitting in the new chair, which groaned as I sat in it. I didn't open the book again, and Brother Jacob did not look away from me.

"Brigid says you have drawn a Divine One to you before?"

I tried to examine his face for expression, but couldn't tell what he thought. Chewing on the inside of my cheek, I said, "There was a unicorn who lived in the...area around the lair."

I avoided saying dragon or dragonhaunt, or referring to Ragnark by name. The brothers sighed or scowled when I did so. It was for the best, so I didn't alarm other people by mistake. They already saw me so seldom that they weren't sure what to think of me.

"How often did you see the Divine One?" Brother Jacob asked.

"Once a month?" I wasn't certain, but that seemed right.

"When was the last time you saw him? Did being with the Dark One taint you?"

Once again he was trying to remind me that dragons weren't animals, but sources of evil. I was glad that Ragnark had taught me how to avoid an argument. It made coping with some of the brothers' lessons easier, at least on my part. For the brothers, it probably made teaching me all the more frustrating. Seeing their frustration was a source of pleasure when I was furious with them and unable to express it.

This time, I frowned and considered not responding to him. Calling Ragnark a Dark One still made my skin crawl, and Brother Jacob's refusal to even say the word 'dragon' rankled. Then I thought about his question and decided I would tell him exactly what had happened the last time I saw a 'Divine One'. I lifted my chin and said, "The last time I saw the unicorn was last Easter. I saw him check on the twins he had sired, then he left. I followed him to where a maiden sat weaving grass."

Brother Jacob had gone still and his folded hands were pale. A ripple of doubt stole through my stomach, but I was drawn into the spell of the story myself. Even if I'd wanted to stop, I couldn't have. I continued, "He approached her and stabbed her through the stomach before you shot him."

Brother Jacob said nothing to confirm or deny my subtle accusation. He didn't move, and I wondered if he was so much as breathing. The fire popped and spat when it hit a sap-ridden log, casting harsh shadows on a face suddenly torn and foreign, a face hard and pained.

I knew that look. That was the expression my heart still held when I thought about the red dragon who had died not too long ago.

"Anna didn't survive, did she?" Now that I thought about it, our losses had been close together. Strange to think we had each been grieving without letting the other know.

"I buried her in the monastery's cemetery three days later." Brother Jacob's voice broke and he rubbed his brow with a shaking hand. "She wasn't pure. She was twenty-some years old. I thought the age of temptation beyond her."

"You have said yourself that temptation is never beyond us."

Brother Jacob gave a smile that was half-approval and half-shame, and somehow wholly hurt. "She swore to me."

Though the pain made him look older, I also saw that without his worry lines, he wouldn't be so old as I had supposed him. Anna would have been a few or several years older than me, and Jacob perhaps several years older than her, maybe not even that much. I knew from observing matchmaking with my sister that they would have been considered acceptable ages. This came together in my mind with the considerable pain he felt over her loss, then that they had shared a house and hunted together.

"You loved her."

It seemed inevitable to me, just as certain to happen in this case as it was in all the stories of kind people who did good deeds and were rewarded with a fruitful marriage. It seemed natural, almost expected. For it to have ended otherwise was what would have struck me as odd. Interesting how I hadn't ever thought about this before.

His voice was hoarse when he said, "You must not speak of such things. I love all God's creatures."

"But you were in love with her."

"You're too young to know." His eyes were hard, dangerous, and in his voice was a challenge to contest him, and a threat if I did. It was the tone Father had used to call us into order or risk a thrashing.

I chose the softest reply I could think of. "Even a babe knows of love."

Brother Jacob let out a heavy sigh and slumped back into his chair. He said, "Before every hunt, I ask the bait a very important question. It is a question I am asking you now: Are you pure?"

The change in topic had me confused. We were discussing being in love, and now he had asked me if I was pure. Was it a way to avoid a sensitive topic? Even I changed the subject when someone started talking about dragons, so I could easily see why Brother Jacob would want to avoid talking about love, and Anna in particular.

Still, there was something in the set of his shoulders. They went stiff as he waited for my answer, and I thought I saw fear creeping back into his gaze. What link was I missing?

Pursing my lips, I asked back, "I thought Brigid was the bait?"

"Brigid was sent for by another village. Now, answer my question: Are you pure?"

I looked into the fire, blue flames licking around blackened logs crumbling into ashes. He was talking yet again about purity, but I had a nagging feeling that our earlier discussion of being in love wasn't completely shelved. How that could be confused me. Love was portrayed as the greatest of all virtues, the foundation for families and homes, then villages and towns and cities. Even the nation was to be founded on a bedrock of love. The lack of purity was shown as the crumbling of that bedrock, a slippery descent into misery and failure. What had one to do with the other? They were opposites.

A log broke in half while I watched, and I remembered multiple references to the *fire of love* and the *hellfire of sin*. What was the difference between a house fire and a fire in the house? What mattered, the fire itself, or the thing that it burned? But how did that relate to love and sin, exactly?

Then I looked back to Brother Jacob. I knew that if Brother Jacob had known Anna wasn't pure, he wouldn't have used her as bait. She'd lied to him. I knew what that felt like. Both to lie and to receive one. "Anna was too ashamed to tell you the truth. She chose to die rather than live with betraying you."

Which meant she'd loved him, too. But I couldn't voice that, not when Brother Jacob swallowed hard and his fingers curled into a fist. "Melody. Answer my question."

He'd taken that in a different way than I'd intended. It made me want to scream. I was close. So very close. Why didn't they tell me? Why wouldn't anyone tell me? I had hoped that my words would shake free a loose comment, but Brother Frances's reminder about a careless word last sermon must still be fresh in Jacob's mind.

My fingers traced the spine of the book, feeling the strings holding the pages together, feeling the kidskin protecting the stories and lore of so many years ago. Incredible, that he could trust me with this but nothing else. Thinking of Brother Frances's sermon reminded me of something. It reminded me of a few words he had told us about preparing to go on the Easter hunt.

I raised my gaze to the bald spot shaved in the center of his head. "Let her go first."

At the time I hadn't thought much about it, but I knew the pain that Brother Jacob was feeling. I knew that if Ragnark had been killed by a hunter, I would have been very angry. Vengeful might be a better word for it. How could I think Brother Jacob would be any less tempted than I would be? And this posed as great a danger to me as the question of my purity to him. Hunting a unicorn with revenge in mind would not sit well with anyone, and I was certain that Brother Jacob would regret it, assuming that we all didn't feel the burn of that mistake.

Brother Jacob's eyes darkened and darted up to meet mine. He said, "What do you mean?"

"You don't trust me. I can see it in your eyes. You don't trust Brigid, either. If you kill the unicorn with hate in your heart, you'll damn yourself, and perhaps me as well."

"Anna, stop with your games," Brother Jacob snapped.

"I'm not Anna," I said. Brother Jacob shut his eyes. He hurt more than I did, and though I wanted to respect that and give him space, our time was short and the stakes may well be my life...if not more than that. The time had come to change the subject. "I want to learn, Brother Jacob. Teach me. I'll do as you say, even hunt unicorn."

Brother Jacob's lips thinned. "I asked you a simple question."

I folded my arms and leaned back, cradling the book against my chest. He wouldn't say anything else of interest. He was through being baited. Now he wanted answers from me. Grudgingly, I said, "I don't know what it means to be anything but pure."

Brother Jacob rubbed his temples. Some of the strain of our conversation disappeared with the wrinkles on his brow. Had he really thought that it was possible for me to not be pure? I couldn't think how, not with how closely they watched me. He stopped rubbing the spot between his brows and rested a finger on his nose. "You always say you want to learn?"

"Yes?"

He said, "I will have tutors brought to you when we return from the hunt."

"Tutors for what?"

"Anything you'd like."

Anything I'd like, except that which would endanger my purity, of course. It was more than training, it was a bargain. Forget this night, stop searching for answers. He was baiting me, no doubt about it. But I could do worse than this life. If I learned other things, I might be able to directly benefit from them. But I wouldn't forget about this puzzle. Across the span of our arms, Brother Jacob watched me consider.

Was this wrong? It felt like it might be, but a poor girl from a mud hovel needed every advantage she could get in life. I met his gaze. "You'd best have tutors arranged. Drawing, painting, book binding, embroidery, record keeping, and whatever else the lord's sons learn. I'll hunt unicorn."

***

I rubbed my fingers over fine tendrils of flame, stopping to warm my toes as well. The hunt was cold, and every evening I saw smoke from a fire Brother Jacob lit for me, though it was small and burned poorly, the wood being wet from a light drizzle which scarcely stopped day and night.

Early spring flowers bobbed next to where I sat on my wool cloak, the petals darkened and crinkled from the ice of last night. We weren't supposed to have a fire at all. The hunt was a time for reflection, a time to abstain from all earthly delights, to be rendered even more pure. In practice it made me feel sympathy for beggars and lepers.

From the phase of the moon, Brother Jacob and I had been on the hunt for nearly a month and a half. He had warned me that my first hunt would take a long time, but I had thought that my past experience would make the unicorn easy to coax. This wasn't so. Tonight had been the first night that I kept the fire burning all night long. I wondered if Brother Jacob was awake yet.

Despite my best efforts to shake him, he had remained on my trail. I wondered if he knew that I was intentionally trying to break free from his shadow, if only for a day, or if he thought I was just following shapes in the mist. One thing I knew now for certain: If I ever acted on my fantasies of running away after a spat, Brother Jacob would find me if he wanted.

I added three sticks to the fire, sticks I had slept with against my side to protect them and perhaps dry them, and I left the fire. I hoped that Brother Jacob would come to the flames and would be distracted while I foraged for food. It was more than just the prospect of being able to run away, though. I had to admit, it was the challenge.

I wanted to outwit him in this game of hunter and prey. Should he have proven easy to get away from, this wouldn't be so entertaining. It gave me something to think about when the waiting grew monotonous. It gave me a way to communicate and interact with him when we couldn't risk letting our scents mingle. My stomach rumbled. Other virgins may be pious and truly fast, but not me. With a bit of regret, I left the warmth of the fire.

My search for food lead me into a still-frozen mire where berry bushes snared skin and cloth alike. Deep into their tearing thorns, I found berries dried upon arched branches. I ate until the backs of my hands bled freely with fine lines from the thorns. I pulled down a branch and heard the distant buzz of bees angry at being disturbed. I jumped, my foot breaking through thin ice and sinking into shallow mud.

Behind me, a large creature snorted. Adrenaline made my body freeze. That snort had come from what, exactly? Bears lived in these woods. They usually did not come out to bother the villages, but they were known to take a hunter's deer or kill his horse and hounds. Of course, they made a good deal of noise in underbrush and I hadn't heard anything. Would I, though? Would I have heard anything over my own snapping and breaking of the wispy arms of berry bushes?

I turned, slowly, and came face to face with a white unicorn the size of a large stag. He blocked my path back out, the white tuft of hair on the end of his tail stuck in the berry thorns. For an instant, I checked on his stance and muscles. Stiff, but his head was raised, nose slightly extended. Had he been The Mule instead, I would have called him curious but nervous. Not threatening, at least not yet. I stood still, unsure if I should try to escape the bees or risk frightening him.

Then I remembered the straw mattress and the pot of sop simmering over the hearth fire waiting for us at home. If Brother Adams had made it, it would be onion cooked until the whole pot was a thick mush, and he would have a loaf of soft flatbread just off the griddle. If Anna had made it, the sop would be a pot of carrots, cooked until their many colors seeped into the water and melded into a brown broth. The bread would be hard and burned, but we'd eat it by crumbling it into the sop and letting it soak. These thoughts eased my pounding heart as I sank slowly to my knees and began to hum.

The bees must have been too cold to find me, since I didn't hear anything else out of them beyond their initial disturbed buzz. Ignoring the unicorn was the best thing I could do for now. Let him see that I wasn't upset over him and he shouldn't be upset over me. After all, he was the one with the horn and I didn't have anything I could use against him. It was the hunter's purpose to claim the blood of the unicorn, and the hunter's purpose to keep the virgin safe.

Where had Brother Jacob gone? Had I lost him, or had my fire worked to mislead him for a while? This timing was inconvenient, but I considered that if I had slipped away from Brother Jacob, then perhaps it was this extra space that the unicorn had been waiting for to approach me. For now, the best I could do was to keep my fingers occupied. When my knees went numb I began to weave a basket out of the brambles I had pulled down, first flicking off the thorns with my nails and stripping them of old and new leaves.

The unicorn's nose was suddenly in my face, smelling my hair. Hot bursts of breath left cold droplets on my neck that I wanted to rub away but didn't dare. I showed him a berry in the palm of my hand. It was dark red against the cream of my skin, still frozen and plump while the others had been shrivelled and dried. The unicorn's ribcage expanded and collapsed when his nose lowered and he took great gulps of the scent. Brown eyes blinked at me, not hungry, but enticed. His lips brushed my palm as he took the berry.

Then he jerked and leapt forward. His body was a

solid mass of taut muscles hurtling for me, his hooves tracing a bolt of light, so white and clean that they looked as though they'd never been in this mire. They came for my face. I rolled under his belly, feeling thorns sink into my side and a hoof collide with my hip. Pressure and the knowledge that my bone would bruise and swell, but no immediate pain. Too many hot flashes bolting through my body for pain. I flipped to see the unicorn, to know which way I'd have to dodge next.

One hoof struck the ground, strong stride, his head high and tail arching through the final swishes of the bound. A fore-hoof touched a patch of grass and his body pivoted away from me. I was climbing to my hands and knees, starting to scurry. He didn't look injured, but maybe I could get away. Then, two steps later, his other foreleg collapsed beneath his weight and he fell to the ground, sprawled in mud and uprooted grass. Breaths heaved on his ribs, and an arrow jutted out of his other side. The breathing stopped, his heart shattered.

My own heart thudded in my ears and white puffs of clouds formed in front of my lips. Steam rose from my knees where I had exposed warmer mud to the cold air. Then the sun emerged from the clouds again and the world was instantly warmer, though despite this I started shaking.

I looked up the hill and found Brother Jacob kneeling on a rock outcropping, hands folded in prayer. It seemed like the next thing to do. I swallowed several times to work moisture into my mouth. I tried to pray likewise, but instead of words, Ragnark's death song was upon my lips. It was thin and breathy, but just doing it soothed the shakes out of my hands and eased the noise of my heart.

Brother Jacob climbed down the side, and he shoved his way through the brambles. He said, "Next time, stay out in the open."

I finished the last of the song. Stood back, holding my elbow in my arm and stroking it for comfort. Brother Jacob, heavier than me, broke through the ice that made the mire stiff. I made no move to immediately help him, looking at his back instead of at the fallen beast. "Do what needs done. I'm ready for a fire and good meal."

When he turned, he was a changed man. He must have found time to shave once or twice, but not recently. The growth of his beard wasn't nearly as disturbing as it was to see the bald spot on his head growing in with dark curls. "Melody. You've just witnessed your first sacrifice."

"My first sacrifice was a lamb slain so I might live. If this creature has died so others may live, then I have no guilt in my heart," I replied, calmly. It was true that I felt the lamb's death more keenly than the death of the unicorn, but I was still unsettled. Not that I wanted to show it.

Brother Jacob's eyes widened, then he shook his head, and said, "I'll need help to pull him out."

There was no arguing there, and now that the unicorn was dead, I wouldn't see him go to waste. I tucked his tail between his legs so it wouldn't drag, then took the unicorn by a back leg and helped Brother Jacob pull. My whole body ached, my hip in particular, by the time we had the unicorn where the horse and mule could approach. We loaded the unicorn on the back of The

Mule, and I rode behind Brother Jacob on his horse.

"What now?" I asked.

"You'll see." Brother Jacob guided his horse in a direction I'd never been before. My wonder was not as strong, though, as the pain in my hip, so I kept quiet and endured the ride.

CHAPTER 8

Within three days we had left behind the wilderness with its clear springs, rough trails, and the sounds of birds following our progress through their territory. The game trails became larger footpaths, which merged with a two-tracked road gouged with wheels, then that road smoothed into a cobbled lane winding between rich people's houses where workers had abandoned their scaffolding and bricks for the Easter rest days.

Brother Jacob lead us to a great house with a tall gate propped open with other cowled men greeting pilgrims. At first I had supposed the place to be a castle, with all the giant stone walls and the garden of herbs and vegetables newly planted that we rode to, but when more monks came out, I knew the place for a monastery. One monk helped me down from the horse, another two spoke to Brother Jacob, and several others took The Mule away with admiration for the unicorn. The process of tending to the unicorn was done outside of my view.

One of the monks tried to coax me into walking with him into a doorway, but I remembered Judas and remained steadfast next to Brother Jacob. The monks then invited him to supper, and the entire party started to move towards a building.

"Melody," said Brother Jacob, pausing in the door. "The refectory is only for monks."

I bit my lip, smelling dowcet custard and currants coming from inside. My eyes stung despite myself, and I muttered softly, "I'll be with The Mule, then."

Supposing I could find the stables, that was. This deep into the monastery, the crowds were thin but it was still a sprawling place with buildings which all had the same design.

Brother Jacob caught my elbow. "Wait. Brothers, is the abbot taking visitors?"

"He just asked to see Melody. I'll take her," said another, elbowing his way to the center of our circle as though he had just come to find us.

I looked at the scrawny man with hair so thin that shaving a bald spot was redundant. I didn't move. Brother Jacob's brow furrowed. "Melody?"

"Will I be safe?" I asked.

Brother Jacob's eyes darted to the man next to me, and a smile broke over his face. "They may well be strangers to you, but they are family to me. Go meet the Abbot. You'll have better food than even I will."

The other monks nodded in agreement. One looked relieved by my caution, while another one steadied his gaze on me suspiciously. The youngest of their number seemed confused by my reluctance. With hardly a glance back, I went with the strange monk. Brother Jacob's word was good enough for me.

The thin-haired monk proved to be as chatty as Brigid,

and I set to following close on his heels, listening to him talk as we walked through busy hallways until we came at last to the Abbot. A rug lay in the middle of the floor, with a table and fine chairs around it.

A kindly man with wrinkles and sagging cheeks greeted me, but the expression of his face was lost in the wealth of his headdress and robes he wore. I supposed that the richness of the monastery and the men inside was intended to be a heaven upon earth, or possibly a way to impress rich folk into greater donations. Though awed by the power of the place, I wished that more of the money that had gone into this monastery had instead been put to use helping those who had nothing.

Nevertheless, the man before me had something about him, some presence that was soothing and welcoming. I'd heard stories of people who could heal just by touching another person, but I'd always dismissed them as tales to inspire hope and nothing more. Deep in my gut, I knew this man was exactly what those stories were about.

Everything about him was fairly normal, average height and weight, pale blue eyes, all normal features, except that when I looked at those hands held out to me, I saw a faint winking of light off his skin. Without a doubt, I knew that this man was a healer, and not like the sort that gave herbs and reasonable advice. Nor was he a healer like the educated physicians who charted the stars and read from books and used leaches. No, this man had a gift to heal from the soul out. I didn't dare tell anyone else this, though. They'd think I was out of sorts. Or, worse, they'd believe me when I could scarcely believe it myself.

"You are welcome, Daughter Melody. I have heard of your bravery, but was not expecting one so young. Come, sit and receive my blessing, eat your fill with me. You have had a trying time."

I shivered despite myself as I sat into a chair heavy and carved, entirely too large for my small body. Though I wanted to look about the room, I couldn't take my eyes off the abbot. Watching him, listening to him, it was like seeing my father bending over a lamb and whispering words to it. Mother had said I mustn't tell anyone, and she had looked afraid when she told me that. But those moments with Father were scarce. This abbot, though...I felt it. Whatever that something was, the abbot always had the healing called about his hands and voice.

Witchcraft. I tried not to think it, and when I did anyway, I was instantly guilty for having thought that about him. But now that I'd labelled it, that was what it was: Magic. The abbot had magic. Healing magic, good stuff that the world needed more of, not bad magic like was implied with witchcraft. And then I realized I'd compared the abbot to my father, which meant...my father had magic, too.

"Are you well, my child?" the abbot asked, responding to my shock.

"I am cold. Hungry." I remembered that I'd said those same words before, when I didn't know what else to say. That didn't make them not true. I was fighting to not declare, *You have magic. I see it. I feel it. Then why is the church so afraid of it?*

"I fear we only have a hearth for cooking. None of the other rooms have fire. But I have something just as well."

The abbot stood, took the outer robes off his own shoulders, and draped them over mine.

Any objections I had were stuck in my throat. Surely this wasn't proper, I shouldn't be wearing the clothes of his station, but surely he had the right to do as he would? In any case, it was warm.

The abbot paused, then reached forward with a shaking hand to feel my forehead. "You are very quiet, my daughter. Are you frightened?"

I tried to smile at him. Shaking on the inside, but the man's peaceful behavior soon calmed my stomach. "No, abbot. I am only a quiet child."

"The meek are the tenderest blessing the Lord gives us in this life. It is a shame they are not more celebrated. You must forgive me, for I am one of those who God made to talk often and in great portions." The abbot continued into a prayer, saying it in the same tone as he did everything else, so I almost missed the call to say Amen. Whatever shock I'd felt was now gone, dismissed with the man's touch, as well as the fear that he or others would find out about my father. I realized the table before us was already set with silver trays of various meals.

The abbot set about serving me heartily from every dish. He wouldn't let me help with anything, taking it upon himself to wait on me. Had it been anyone else, I would have felt uncomfortable and embarrassed, like I was out of my station. But with him, I knew it was his duty, and the only thing he wanted of me was for me to be gracious. He served me cockles and whelks, eel and sole, umbles, and finally the dowcet.

We had ale with the meal, and it was an ale so smooth and thick I thought it was some other drink new to me. He admitted that this was almost a feast, but he had been so well-pleased with the reports of me that he felt I deserved an early treat.

"Tomorrow," he promised. "You will have our wine."

I ate beyond the point of being full, as I had seldom done before. The food was so plenty and so rich, I felt it would be an insult to leave even a bite remaining. All the while, the abbot talked, but I couldn't say what about. Nothing of importance. Just bits and pieces about life, fondly remembered stories, the occasional tale about a man who had made him laugh. Then he mopped up a small spill I'd made with the ale, and his eyes caught mine.

The abbot suddenly looked serious. "How do Brothers Adams and Jacob treat you? Are they keeping you well?"

I wondered if he was asking me another question entirely, but couldn't determine what it was. A few seconds went by, then I said, "They act like two fathers."

Relief washed over the man's wrinkled brow, smoothing it out. He said, "And how did you find your first hunt? Most girls find it to be a little distressing."

"I was prepared for it."

The abbot nodded. "And the dragon you had been with? How was your time with him?"

"The brothers call him the Dark One."

"I call him a dragon. Nothing more or less than another creature inhabiting this existence."

I raised my gaze to his, surprised by his admission. It was hard to tell what he wanted me to say, and I thought this was part of the way he was getting to know me. "He was my teacher. He taught me the stories of pagans."

There was no look of horror, nor any revulsion in the abbot's eyes. Emboldened, I continued, "The brothers wouldn't want to hear of that, either, but I am glad Ragnark told me the tales. One day there was a bonfire where the villages left their offerings for me, and I went down to it while it was still burning well. Ragnark warned me to wait, but I didn't. And a man was there, waiting for me. He said his name was Judas and that he was a Godian and he would take me. He frightened me so I ran. He found me, but Ragnark came and killed him."

The abbot closed his eyes and his lips moved in quiet words, but he wasn't stopping my story. Before this, I hadn't ever wanted to relate the events of that day, but now...now I needed to. It felt good and painful to revisit Ragnark in my memories.

"I wouldn't have known the man was not Godian, except for the way Ragnark had taught me to identify the others. He saved me more than once that day." I paused, then asked, "What did the man mean when he said that?"

The abbot opened his eyes, and I now realized that they weren't pale blue, but were brown with whitish-blue spots over them. He said, "The man meant to take your virtue. But you do not know what that means, do you? So much the better, my daughter. Now you listen well to what I say: Do not repeat your story to anyone else, and do not speak again of Ragnark."

"Why?"

The abbot smiled at me. "You thirst for knowledge and understanding in a world where it is not always to be had. It is as God has created you, and so I will not attempt to hamper it, only shape it. Others do not have a mind like we do. People want comfort and security, for so much in this world is uncertain and uncertainty is frightening. The dragon is the shape Lucifer took, and so the dragon is evil. The unicorn is pure and clean, and every year it sacrifices itself for us, the same as our Lord and Savior has done, and so the unicorn is divine and good."

My brow narrowed. "But Lucifer didn't only take the shape of a dragon. He took many forms."

"But the dragon is the most frightening, is it not?"

I sighed.

The abbot leaned forward and rested his hand on mine. "If others were to hear of Ragnark saving you, they would fear you, not the dragon. Indeed your quiet manner and mysterious ways leave much room for fear. Particularly when coupled with your keen observation, the way you notice things that everyone else sees but takes no heed of. I understand the workings of your mind, but others will not and do not. If they think your gifts come from God, you will be treasured. If they think your gifts come from elsewhere, you will be shunned. Take heart: You are blessed with your mind and your manners. I ask you to be wise and know when to use which one."

I nodded, upset by what he was saying and confused. For the same reason I couldn't tell my bones to grow taller than Brigid, neither could I tell other people to grow more brains in their skull. But why did they fear me? What was there to fear in a girl smaller than others her age, and a girl besides?

"It will make sense in time."

I nodded again. Perhaps, if I was as keen as he thought I was, I would. But for now, it didn't make sense. For now it was a weight about my neck and a cloud in my mind.

The abbot said, "My daughter, you know dragons best. I ask of you, would you be willing to go to other dragons when they call for a sacrifice?"

I lifted my gaze and said, "Yes. I want to go."

I knew how to talk with a dragon. I knew how to live on my own, how to make do in a tight situation, and how to rely on my own wits. Here, in this land of people with their strange ways and their constant fear, I was a foreigner. And more than that, I had to pretend to be one of them, hiding myself in the process. A dragon would be a relief.

He studied my face and gave a slow nod. "Very well. But should you choose to not go, know that you have already earned my undying respect and love, and I will forever hold you in my heart as a cherished daughter."

"Thank you," I said, unsure of what else to say, and thinking that I would never refuse to see a dragon, my mind spinning over what we had spoken about.

After supper with the abbot, I was permitted to wander the monastery without an escort. People were everywhere from all walks of life. There were miners and farmers and fishmonger's wives, there were beggars and pilgrims and more. Eventually, I stopped identifying people by their trades, and started to look for anyone that I recognized. I was ready to go some place quiet to rest.

At the guest quarters, I saw Brigid. I smiled and began

to make my way over to her, dodging busy monks and others, but I stopped. She was talking to someone, a boy a year or two older than her, and she was grinning so broadly at him that her skin seemed to glow. She and the boy slipped back into a corner, trying to gain a measure of privacy. The anonymity of two young faces in a crowd of pilgrims was probably the only way they could speak to each other without meeting the scowling disapproval of the brothers.

I sighed to myself and decided I would speak with her after a walk through the gardens. By the time I returned, she was already gone, and the boy with her.

CHAPTER 9

One day, Lord Richmond's man came back to the cottage while I weeded the garden with Brother Jacob. I had only to look at the red horse and the spare white mare who walked alongside to know that a dragon had come calling. While Brother Jacob and the man talked, I went to pack a basket and fetch The Mule.

With nothing more than a short farewell to the cottage occupants, I mounted the white mare brought by Richmond's man, and I rode away, leaving behind a house doubtless little less distressed and shocked than the first time I had done this. The Mule came with me, as he always did. We rode day and night, stopping when The Mule locked its knees and refused to move. We would let the horses rest, and when The Mule was ready to travel, we went on the trails again.

In time we came to a valley entirely different from what I had been used to, if indeed this landscape could be called a valley at all. Once I had heard the term 'canyon', and I could only suppose that this was a canyon. Unlike Ragnark's mountains, there was no prominent mountain where a lair might be; instead, there was a wall of cliffs with water spilling down the sides. Below the cliffs were swamps and creeks which sloped down into a thick river. Though willow and various other plants lined the river, on the other side was a dry landscape with thin vegetation and scattered scrawny trees.

Noble rode away, leaving me to wonder where it was that the dragon had his lair. I looked to The Mule, who shook his head and let his ears flap against my shoulder, then he put one hoof down on the powdery dust of a trail swooping down to the valley. It seemed like as good of a direction as any. Once we dropped below the rim, we walked by clear water dribbling down stones and dripping in fern-lined pools where songbirds landed to flutter their feathers and splash. When the trail finished winding back on itself and finally flattened out alongside a creek, tiny insects came out to feast on whatever flesh wasn't covered.

I stopped to light a smokey fire when the sun dropped over the rim and shadows made me shiver and the bugs come out in swarms. When I had a knee-tall fire spewing black smoke so thick it made my throat ache, The Mule discovered its repellent properties and pushed me out of the smoke. Though I could breathe easier, I found that by the second breath, I was inhaling bugs. I shoved The Mule back, and he flattened his ears and quivered his lip. I pushed him harder, and soon our fight became slap-for-bite.

There came a swoosh of air and the crack of willow branches breaking across from the fire from us, and The Mule and I both jumped and peered through thick smoke to see a slender dragon taking shape in the mud before us, folding his wings against his back and blinking in the smoke. The Mule flattened his ears and took two challenging steps towards him, baring his teeth, and I clutched my thin cloak in my spare hand, calming a beating heart.

The dragon shook his head, and the shake shivered down his whole body, stopping at a thrashing tail which upended a young birch tree. He yawned, then looked down to me.

He was the size of the Brother's cottage, and his cheekbones ended in frills. Though he was far smaller than Ragnark had been, his scales shined bright as though oiled, and in his movements were the quick jerks of a young dragon.

I called up to him, "Hello, my name is—"

"I know what you are, Child of Earth. What have you come to offer me?" His voice, like the twitch of his claw as he scratched his leg, was fast and smooth.

I worried for his turn of mind and the way he seemed to be able to think fast. I was going to have to match him point for point, the way I occasionally had with Ragnark when he quizzed me. Holding both my hands behind my back so they would not shake, I said, "What is it you would like to be offered?"

A silken chuckle came from his throat, and he lowered his head, winding his long neck around a willow to look at me from behind. "There is nothing I want that I do not have. Nothing but..." He drew his head back, lifted it high in the air and cocked his head to the side. "...

amusement. Tell me, Child of Earth, what is it *you* would like offered more than anything else in the world?"

My heart skipped and I was suddenly bewildered.

"...That is," the dragon said, "What is it that I may easily give you?"

I studied his scales and bit my tongue. He was a fire dragon. But I didn't want to offend him, not so early in our acquaintance. I said, "Perhaps I might ask first, what is the price I must pay for such consideration?"

Smoke frothed from the corners of his mouth and he said, "Well, well. A thorough and intelligent human." The dragon looked out to the dry landscape beyond the river. "Cross it barefoot, and I will grant you whatever I may."

That was suspicious, and I wondered if there was an enchantment of sorts on the land—but then the dragon crouched, and launched straight into the air. Three beats of his wings later, he was soaring for the dry grasses— and I realized as fire issued from his mouth what the task would be.

Only weeks before, I had heard Brother Adams speaking of how to cross a river of ice—very slowly, very carefully, preferably while crawling.

The dry trees erupted into flames.

This was not ice. It was fire.

The dragon wanted me to cross over fire. I looked to The Mule as the hillside caught ablaze, fire crawling away from the dragon's initial line of flames, leaping from one tree limb to another. The Mule yawned, waving his tongue in the air, then closed his mouth and ground his teeth. He stepped back into the smoke.

I watched as the dragon darted to a dark space on the cliffs. "Yeah," I muttered. "It isn't all that impressive, is it?" Then, I pushed my way under his chin and hid from the insects again.

First light saw me examining the burn with The Mule grazing not far away. The fire was still burning in some places, but I went to where the dragon had first started his fire, and noticed that it was a thin strip from one creek to another, perhaps ten times the height of my body. Everywhere the dragon fire had been, pebbles had turned into bubbles and large rocks had a rough, charred crust on them.

"That is one bored dragon," I said to The Mule as I took hard bread from his tack.

The Mule responded by smelling my bread and twitching his lips. I broke the loaf into pieces and fed him one off the palm of my hand. He drooled as he chewed.

I looked back out to the flames. "Is it bad I'm even considering this?"

The Mule bobbed his head, but I couldn't be sure if that was a genuine response, or just him working bread around his mouth.

Kneeling down, I held my hand over the nearest coals. They were hot enough they'd raise blisters if I held my hand there. I shook my head and stepped back, instead studying the cliffs for a way to the dragon's lair.

I went that night to the fire dragon's lair without having so much as attempted the feat.

The dragon had been watching me. His yellow eyes focused on mine, then he let out a snort and said, "I suppose you are only a child of the earth.'"

With a heavy scrape of his armored tail against stone rubbed smooth by his scales, he turned his back on me, blocking entrance to the lair. Spirited with the weariness of the picking a path through the cliff side, I snapped at his retreating tail, "I never pretended to be anything else!"

The dragon gave me no reply. Thus my night was spent next to The Mule and in ill-humor, disturbed by racing dreams and memories of dares with my siblings.

When dawn found us, the fire dragon seemed to have overcome whatever disappointment he had felt by my behavior, but my indignant emotions had stewed into something much more potent, a mixture of anger and determination. The fire dragon yawned and hummed a, "Good morning, childhe," at me, but I only stood up in the growing light and glared at him.

Then I turned on my heel and left.

I was going to find a way to cross those coals without his help, because at this very moment, I hated him. I hated him for...for what, exactly? My brow knit, then I lifted up my chin. I didn't know what for, but I was still going to cross those coals.

I had walked barefoot on a variety of surfaces, but never before coals—well, not a lot of them. Fires are sloppy by nature, spitting out coals and sparks at will, so it was inevitable that I had trod on a few coals during the course of my life.

When I reached the ring where blackened remains of fire still spouted the occasional tongue of flame, I had not come up with a satisfactory manner to so much as put my foot down, much less complete a full walk. I sat down upon a rock and thought, remembering how my mother would remove cooked items from the fire, how she was giving my sister instruction in how not to burn her finger next time.

"Move quickly, but not too fast. Grasp it firmly enough to lift it up, but no more. Do either of these too roughly and you will burn yourself. Move too slow and you will burn yourself. Try it."

My sister, still nursing a red spot on her thumb, objected that it was not possible.

"Not possible?" My mother sighed. "Then how did I feed this rabble for twenty years?"

Never one to be left out of a lesson or shine when my siblings could not, I promptly removed the baked bread the first time.

Mother had spared a sigh and a glare for me. I had always been her most independent child, a characteristic I took pride in while the rest of the world groaned.

To fill the place where praise should have been, I spread out my fingers in display, and said, "See? It's possible."

This started a fight with my sister, but I was now trying to understand how that had worked to not burn my fingers.

After a while of going no where, I decided to try walking on the cooler ground, the part where the fire had died off first. By walking on the warmer places, the places which would burn if I were to stand still, I learned how to walk evenly on my feet, how to be brisk yet not run.

I still burned the arch of my foot when a coal stuck to my skin, and received an extra burn on my other foot when I brushed the offending coal away and put too much weight on a single foot. Nevertheless, I did make it to the other side of the ring....and I didn't desire much to go back. Nursing my feet in the cold of a spring, I waited for the coals to die.

The fire dragon, at about midday, wandered to where I sat wrapping my feet up in torn shreds of my under dress.

"You are no child of the earth," the dragon said, sounding fascinated and confused. "But nor are you a child of the fire. The fire is drawn to you, though, and the darkness looks away."

He turned his head this way and that, then he asked, "What gift would you have asked of me?"

I bit my lip, angry that I had been denied a prize by the misfortune of an accident, but somewhat soothed with the admiration I had gained in the dragon's eyes. My voice was decisive when I said, "I want a scale. One which has a good curve in the center, like one on the ridge of your neck."

Black pupil overtook his orange iris in surprise. "Why do you want a scale? I might have given you any of the gems in my hoard. I would have given you a taste of my blood, which would have let your body heal quickly, or I would have taught you magic to learn any language. Would you still have a scale?"

I folded my hands in my lap, sitting cross legged before him on a boulder as the sun parted clouds and basked me in its rays until the dragon shifted and cast me into shadow. I could have received such boons from any dragon, but the same way that one does not compare friends to each other, one does not hint that there might be other dragons in a virgin's life. Fire dragons were common enough, but I had no assurances of seeing another one this far north.

"I am often used as bait," I said instead. "I cannot light a flame without scaring away the prey."

The fire dragon turned a golden eye, dashed with hints of silver, to examine me and said, "You are speaking of the Easter Unicorn hunt?"

"I am."

A slitted eye blinked, and I had no idea if he thought this was reprehensible, or if it was a joyous pursuit as some dragons loathed the unicorn, or if he saw my role in a more practical light. I was surprised when the dragon said, "Is not the cold and absence of food essential to cleanse yourself to be the bait?"

According to Ragnark's tales and commentary, dragons cared little to understand the ways of man. The fire dragon's knowledge impressed and confused me, but I knew better than to try to underscore this dragon's intelligence by pretending his knowledge was wrong. Brutality came through my voice, as this topic had been an argument Brother Adams had dismissed mere days before coming to the fire dragon.

"Penance is one concept; dying from the night and the cold is simply a poor idea."

Smoke rolled out of the dragon's nostrils and from around his lips as he tried to not laugh. I never could guess what was going on in his head.

"Who told you about my scales?"

"It was in a story."

Watery eyes shimmering in the flickering daylight stared at me, unanswering. A cloud of black smoke came from the dragon's nostrils, darker than usual and smelling more potently of sulfur. When the sky had shifted to purples and pinks, the fire dragon said, "My scales do indeed warm as stated, but remember, warm to a dragon is the red of iron. I suppose the scale you have requested will scorch meat, boil water, heat metal, and start fires. It would have its uses for your situation—but what would be better is to take a unicorn hide. With that you would be neither hot nor cold whilst you wear it. You will have to steal the hide, for rest assured, the church will not willingly part with it, and you must forever keep it from discovery. Sew seams into it to appear as though it is made from hares, and it will fool most humans."

He gave me the scale as a parting gift when I left him after four months of being his captive. The scale was a young scale, strong and small and with the ability to become very, very hot. Unlike the cast-off scales which looked like the cracked remains of an oyster shell, rough on one side and polished on the other, this scale clearly looked draconic. Though small, it was nevertheless the length of my forearm.

When Noble and I were a day's ride away from the dragon, I said, "I heard rumor that the monks fashion the unicorn hide into various items."

Noble jumped, unaccustomed to hearing me speak. He said, "Yes?"

"What do they do with the scraps?"

"Why?" He asked, pulling his horse up short to look at me.

I lifted my chin and said, "I want to make a cloak of them. It gets cold, and I'm sure the Abbot wouldn't want me to freeze from exposure next time."

Noble looked me head to toe and said, "I will speak to him for you."

We started home again.

CHAPTER 10

Brother Jacob opened the door for me, looking at my escort, his face slackened and pale, as though he had been worried. Snow was falling behind us, and Brother Jacob said, "Come inside, quickly. We have fresh clothes waiting for you both."

I eagerly changed out of my dragon-scented clothes, careful to keep the scale hidden from view. Brigid hugged me at the first chance she had.

"It is good to have you home. I suppose you'll sleep well tonight?"

I laughed, "I hope so! This last one made certain to always have me on my toes."

Brigid gave a nervous laugh, "I hope you do sleep, then."

She wouldn't meet my gaze. Had she seen my dragon scale?

"Brigid, is there something you want to talk about?" I asked, trying to think of a way to explain.

"No, why?" she asked, then forced a smile. "But listen to me standing here talking to you. You must be hungry. There's chicken in the pot tonight. The woman who has all the hens? She told her husband that if he wouldn't fix the thatching before the first snow, she wouldn't feed him anything from the hen house, and now we have meat!"

With that, Brigid lead the way to the fire. I hoped that meant she wasn't going to announce what she had seen before everyone.

Brother Adams and my escort did most of the talking that night. For once Brigid was silent, and for all the way she had spoken of supper, she ate less than I remembered her eating. The abbot had sent the brothers several gallons of monastery ale, and we drank from that until my eyelids were heavy, and everyone went to bed.

As I had grown accustomed to doing, I woke during the night, startled at first to see the darkness of the cottage and smell wood smoke. When I recognized where I was, I tried to fall asleep—it was cold despite the coals glowing in the hearth—but something kept me awake. I sat up, and saw that Brigid's mattress beside mine was empty. Slowly, I stood up and pulled on a cloak.

Outside the snow had fallen to be three inches deep. The moon was now out, casting the world in silver-white light. My breath fogged before my lips, and I walked in Brigid's footsteps. A light dusting of snow had fallen over them, so it might have been some time since she had left.

A short walk later, when my nose was growing cold and my toes damp, I stood outside a long-forgotten beggar's shack with smoke puffing out from crack where the mud had fallen away, showing the weaving of willow sticks.

I reached for the door, wondering why Brigid had gone

away in the night, but a male voice stopped my hand. Brigid answered.

I couldn't make out what it was they were saying, but whatever it was, they had not wanted an audience. Ashamed, though I couldn't say why, I backed away and returned to the cottage, walking in the same footprints as the one Brigid had made.

When I took off my cloak and boots inside the brother's cottage, I wondered about waking someone. But I thought about the chaos that would follow, and the thought of Brigid being interrupted by the monks, or worse, the lord's man, and my cheeks heated.

No, I wouldn't tell the others about her, but as I laid down, I couldn't sleep, either.

Some time later, the cottage door opened and Brigid entered. I saw her stop by the fire and poke at it with a stick, stirring life back to it, adding wood distantly around it to dry.

"Brigid," I whispered.

She squinted at me, and lifted a log. "I got fire wood."

I shook my head. "Lace up your sides."

She turned away from me and hastened to do just that.

The next morning, Brigid didn't speak to me any more than was needed to be polite. I tried a few times to coax her into speaking with me, but she wouldn't.

One June morning, I woke when the fire had died and frost had stiffened my blanket, only to find that my rags had soaked through and my underdress was soiled. To my relief, it was still well before the brothers awoke, but my cheeks burned with mortification. How would I stand a lifetime of this? Last month hadn't been so heavy, only a spot and a streak, but this month it was as though I had sat down on a blade and the wound refused to stop bleeding.

Though I searched my memory for the conversation my mother had given my older sisters, I hadn't been paying attention at the time. Now I wished I hadn't been playing with dolls made of sticks and yarn dresses. I gritted my teeth, knowing that I needed to clean my garment, and the sooner the better, but my spare underdress was in a chest which creaked.

As I slipped out of bed, my skin prickled and I shivered. With a glance at the brothers sleeping on the other side of the cottage, I steeled myself and opened the chest as usual. It groaned, ending in a mouse-like squeak. I froze. Brother Jacob's snores fell out of order then resumed as usual, and Brother Adams grumbled and turned to face the wall.

My fingers found my clean underdress, my cheeks burning even though I hadn't been caught in bloody linen. When I closed the chest, I realized I needed to check the mattress, too. There was a spot, not much of one, but I'd need to open up the seam and take out some straw or it would smell wretched in a week. How would I ensure I wasn't in this situation again next month, or for that matter, even tomorrow? Brigid never had these accidents. I shook her awake.

After a few tries, she cracked one eye open. Rubbing her nose, she mumbled, "What?"

"Get up and come with me." It was not a courteous way to ask for help, but it was the shortest.

She squinted in what was either a waking-up examination of the room or a glare at me. "It's too early."

The blush crossed my cheeks again and made talking hard. "I'm bleeding a lot." I sounded scared. I realized I was.

She blinked and scrubbed at her eyes, then glanced at the brothers and swung her legs out of the blanket. Her toes curled when they touched the reed mat. "Got rags?"

I nodded but couldn't admit that I was not sure how to use them. She stood and wrapped her blanket around her torso, a thing I did not do in case anyone saw the stain on the mattress.

We snuck outside, minding the spot where the door moaned, and then headed for the creek lined with a pebble bottom and swollen with snow melting off mountains above. Brigid stood at the edge of the water, arms crossed as she tried not to shake while fog rolled around us. I waded up to my calves in water as cold as a hundred tiny needles, to the depression we'd made with a ring of rocks. It was our usual kettle-filling and cauldron-scrubbing spot, farther away from the shore now that the creek flowed faster.

I undressed, shuddering at the bite of fog, and scrubbed the linen with fingernails. My toes went red and stinging, then my fingers went numb.

"You should wash, too," Brigid said, her voice shivering even as she kept her teeth from chattering.

I jumped when icy water slid down my legs, but set my jaw and splashed water again and again, until I was clean. "How much of this is normal?"

Brigid tried to shrug, succeeding only in shaking from

head to toe. "A day or two. A week or two. A little bit that doesn't hurt at all. A lot that gives you stomach cramps that lays you flat on your back. It's all normal." She paused, watching as I tried time after time to wrap the rags about my body. "You never had this before?"

I didn't answer, suddenly feeling inadequate.

Brigid passed me the clean underdress. "You're old for this. I got mine when I was thirteen, but I was early. You're what, fifteen? Sixteen?"

My cheeks were on fire again and I wished that I hadn't woken her up. "Mother said we would be fourteen when we bled."

Brigid stared at my chest and hips. I wanted to hide, or to scold her for staring, though her looking at me had never bothered me before. She shook her head. "Nah, you're older than that. Don't you keep track of your age?"

"I have a hard enough time keeping track of the months," I grumbled. The truth was, I didn't care about the passage of time. Each morning the sun rose, reached its zenith, and then it sank and night came, and with the night came the moon and stars. Seasons passed. Crops and animals grew and birthed and died. What was the use of attaching a number to those years? In my opinion, the men who counted the days were the laziest among all creatures. It was those who didn't number the years who accomplished the most.

Brigid snickered, rubbing her arms briskly now and shifting on her bare feet. "That will be easy now."

I threw the wet underdress down at her feet, splashing her toes and eliciting a shriek. "No one wants to tell me anything, not even this. I'm not stupid, Brigid, and I'm not delicate."

The smugness, the amusement, all of it went from Brigid's face and she stood before me with slackened mouth and closed eyes. She opened them and sighed. "That's the problem, Melody, you're too smart. When you learn something, you want to know about it all. You face dragons and kill unicorns and you don't shed a tear. You never have hysterics and you seldom laugh. You walk for days and can outwork a mule. The only thing that separates you from a heathen woman is your morals and belief." She stepped closer to me, handing me the wet garment with the words, "Cleave to them, Melody, and stop questioning the one in Heaven. Stop questioning the brothers. Trust them. They know what's best."

I swallowed my resentment but it stuck in my throat. I couldn't put into words what I wanted to say.

Brigid continued. "Last night, Brother Adams said that taming you was the Holy One's greatest victory in the land today. Everyone says so, even those in the church. Pity you don't go more often, but—"

"—I don't like the crowds. All those people crammed shoulder to shoulder in a wood building with candles everywhere. I can't breathe. And they smell." I felt my skin crawl at the memories of sweating through services.

"I know, and there are some in the congregation too loose-lipped to be next to you, anyway."

My eyes slanted at her. "But not too loose-lipped for you?"

The corner of her mouth twisted. "They talk but it doesn't make sense. But you'd put it together. I know you would. Even the innkeeper's wife says so. Not me, though. I need to be shown things."

"But they treat you normal," I snapped. "When I enter a room they all go quiet. And sometimes I say things and they laugh at me. If I'm so smart, why are they laughing?"

Brigid's cheeks turned color and her eyes narrowed. "If you're treated so badly, why don't you leave? You're always saying how you can live all by yourself, why you don't you do it?"

I felt as though she had pushed me into the creek. I looked to the ground. "Because then you wouldn't be with me."

Her jaw dropped but no sound came.

I drew in the pebbles with my toes. "You're the only person who understands me, Brigid."

She let out a long breath, then there was the warmth of her arm over my shoulders. Slowly, we made our way back to the cottage. I stopped in front of the door. "I don't understand, Brigid. Why does this happen to women but not to men?"

Brigid smiled. "You remember reading in the first book. It's an atonement for our great-mother leading us into sin."

I shook my head. "But the female of all animals has the offspring and it's painful for them, too. I think this bleeding is like that, but there's no baby and it doesn't hurt as much."

Brigid's smile was gone, replaced by a pinched brow and a scowl. "How?"

"I don't know. Maybe if—"

She pulled away from me. "No. I won't tell you anything else, but you're wrong. You always do this. You try to make sense of things. Don't do it this time. Anna tried that and look what happened to her. When she was gone, I thought I'd be noticed, then you came along and you're—sometimes. Sometimes when you're like this, I don't know who it is I am talking to." Her face hardened. "I hate you when you're like her. Is it too much to ask that you just be normal? Please, it is so much better for us all when you stop trying to impress people with your questions."

I bit my tongue, horror stopping my heart. Brigid went inside the cottage, leaving the door open a crack. I stared at the hatch marks in the wood from when the lumber had been milled. I whispered to the straw roof, "But that's when I'm me.

Though I hated the idea of going back into the cottage, I needed to take a walk and I couldn't do that without my wool overdress. After a second, I hung my dripping underdress over a low branch which would get the morning sun. I crept through the door. Inside, Brigid was facing the wall, stiff beneath her blanket as she pretended to sleep. I put on my silvery blue dress and brown leather boots, then left again before anyone could wake and discover our quarrel. As I went back out into the fog, I knew they'd be angry with me for not telling anyone where I was going or when I'd be back.

I walked faster, the cold fog stinging down my throat, my numb fingers prickling back to life as I warmed them up in my armpits. They should be wondering *if* I'd be back.

Sticks broke under my careless steps and my boots made stones skitter off the path and into a drainage ditch full of runoff water. Brigid's words buzzed through my ears, leaving and returning from time to time like a wasp flying about my head on a sunny afternoon. I glanced at the softening sky. This place was probably the only place in the kingdom where a person could get frostbitten toes and sunburned arms in the same day. Pain, like an ache with a point on the end, seized my abdomen and I steadied myself on a birch trunk.

Two weeks? Brigid said I could be like this for two weeks? I hoped it would be closer to two days. Then I remembered what she had said about wanting me to be normal, to be less like Anna and more, what? More subdued? More like her? But I couldn't be like Brigid. It would eat me away, slowly but surely. My heart sank just thinking of being like her, idly chatting away about wrens and rabbit holes and repeating stories told weeks ago at worship. It must be nice to have a skull so entirely vacant.

I regretted the thought the instant I let it slip, envisioning how pained it would make Brigid if she knew what I thought of her.

"Brigid, do we like each other at all?" I asked a squirrel grooming her wheat-hued tail. The squirrel blinked at me, her eyes like oiled black beans. My mouth watered when I saw the plump belly and envisioned it dressed and stuffed and roasting over coals, a delicacy Mother made on the days when us girls had success with snares on tree trunks. It was considered poor man's food, and the brothers wouldn't tolerate it, but I had a fondness for stuffed squirrel. We used to sell the hides to line fine ladies' cloaks. For a minute I wondered if I could live on that—eating squirrel and selling the hides. I dismissed the thought. I was prime age to seek a husband. No one in this village, though, they were either married or were still children themselves.

I realized something and laughed, startling a songbird into silence.

What did I think of that? I was a woman now. I was a woman entirely, officially. It was what Mother had said to soothe my distressed older sister Mary when she had gone through this. Mother had said they would watch for a husband, and then they'd have children, but meanwhile Mary would tend to the flocks as usual. From then on, she didn't have to ask permission to do anything or go anywhere. It was the privilege and responsibility of being a woman. My sister had changed after that day, but it was hard to describe that change. She had stood taller, smiled softer, jumped around less. She'd become more graceful. And it had made her think she was too old to be with me anymore, always out talking with journeymen and young merchants. I considered following her example.

It made sense. With the brothers, I was fed, clothed, protected, and educated. Men liked a well-fed woman, and all the better if she had fresh dresses. I smiled at the thought of meeting a man like Allie's blacksmith, and then I wondered how many babies they'd had by now. Four or five, perhaps? Had other sisters found bridegrooms? When would it be my turn? I went to the ditch and viewed my reflection. Freckled cheeks, bright eyes, straight teeth, pudgy face. I was no great beauty, but I was no snaggletoothed hag, either. Maybe I'd turn a head or two.

I watched a green leaf drift by, disrupting my mirror. Prettier women had yet to find husbands, what chance did I have? Ah, well. I couldn't see myself weaving my day away between feeding children. But this thought was nothing more than a consolation. I trudged back on the trail. One way or another, being with the brothers was safe, at least. I saw beggar women and knew they came from places with no father or husband. Best to remain where I was and tolerate Brigid's jealousy until I found some place better.

I heard the pounding of hooves—a horse cantering—and then a snap of a tree limb followed by a thump and a yell. The hooves changed pattern, possibly bucking or playing, and then came a crash of an animal in the underbrush and the slurp of hooves in mud. One of the farmers had a new horse; I remembered Brigid describing its bay color and white star on its forehead.

Hurrying, I jogged through the woods until I came upon a black horse kicking and reeling in circles around a glen, sending a pot tied to his saddle slapping his rump with every hop. It was a young horse, perhaps two years old and long-limbed with a heavy head, braided mane, and uneven coat.

I nearly tripped over the rider. On the ground, shaking twigs out of his dark hair, was a lean man wearing brown trousers. I would have slipped away, but on the back of his neck exposed by his current antics was the same mark that Noble had on his saddle. Mages had those marks, ink drawn on skin then driven into flesh with needles after they passed an initiation rite. This mark was red and raised, partly healed, as though it had been recently made. If he was newly on his own, then the youthful horse and his less than competent relationship with it made sense. I'd never seen a mage before, at least not up close, though I had once spied a cloaked man with a gray beard as he spoke with the sheriff of a town we had passed though.

The man jumped, seeing my boots, and he stared up at me. Green eyes like moss at the bottom of a lake met mine. His skin was dark as old sap, darker than exposure to the sun, his face was lined from the hardships of travel, dust smearing one side of his face and down his tunic. Those eyes glanced at my dress, possibly discerning my station, noting my uncovered hair and the fullness of my skirt. It marked me as a maiden, and one of some status. The cut was similar to the ones the lesser noble maids wore, but the embroidery I had on the hem was done in a similar color to the fabric so it would be modest enough for the brothers. I guessed the mage's age to be early twenties. Young for his occupation, when mages typically did not earn their marks until near thirty. He climbed to his feet, cautiously.

"Are you fairy or nixie?" His voice, like his words, caught me off-guard. The rise and fall of the sounds were musical, light, almost foreign, at once soft yet crisp. Those words strummed across my skin and stirred my stomach, sending a flush of warmth through my body. I loved the feel of his voice and the look in his eyes, the wary yet confident expression of a dominant male crossing a stranger's territory. This was my land, and he knew it the same way a wandering stag knew when he was face to face with the defender of the woods. I wanted to be with this mage longer, but worry nagged at me, that I would make him laugh at me, that I would lose the appreciation in his gaze. So I merely cocked my head at him and said nothing.

He rubbed dust and fragments of pebbles off his clothes. "Might I have your name?"

A smile touched my lips as I noted that like me he was a little awkward in his skin. I remembered something Ragnark had mentioned once. "Mage, why would I give you the one power I truly own?"

His lips parted and his brow raised. "Your name is only the start of your power. Don't you know?" There was wonder in his eyes. "But I would earn your name instead of being given it. What would you have me do?"

I chuckled, both suspicious and charmed. "I would have you bring your horse back to you. Kneel down in the glen where your steed is racing."

The mage's eyes softened. "Ah, but that is something for myself. What may I do for you? What do you desire?"

I extended my arms to feel the air beneath them, not minding the cold with the heat coursing though my body. I motioned around us. "I am here. There is nothing more I wish for."

"Nothing?"

"Nothing."

His lip quirked. "What if I were to tell you there was something more?"

My thoughts went back to Judas, but when I looked at the mage before me, I felt none of the uncomfortableness

I remembered. Being before the mage didn't make me feel like prey to be hunted, but like a host to be respected. It made me feel like a prize fox taunting a hound who had lost his way. "I would tell you that you would have to show me, otherwise I won't believe you."

The mage dipped his head, slight color on his cheeks before he looked to where his horse ran circles between blackberry bushes. My embarrassed laugh brought his attention back to me.

"What a strange conversation I start with you," I said.

"Nonsense. Your side of the talking is very reasonable. It is I who says the odd things. Yet you do not leave."

"I often entertain odd conversations," I said, feeling self-conscious as I remembered Brigid's comments.

Once again his eyes were on me. "A beautiful body is an ugly thing, for it blinds a man to the brilliance of the person before him."

I blushed hotly. "Are you calling me ugly?"

"I'm calling you the shine of light off water, the blanket of snow after a storm, the stars on a moonless night."

Was he true with his praises? Or were they praises at all? Heat spread down my neck. "Do not flatter me so."

"Flattering? Are not the light, the snow, and the stars all capable of blinding and disarming a man? Do not think I flatter you. I admire and respect you. It is entirely different from flattery." With that, he let a brow travel to his hairline. "You told me to kneel?"

I tucked my chin to my shoulder, trying to hide a blush creeping down my neck. "Yes, you can catch anything like that. Cattle, sheep...runaway horses."

The mage's eyes took a mischievous gleam, widening and contrasting with his walnut hued skin. "And what of fairies and nixies?"

I wanted to reach for the twigs in his hair, to cup his cheek in my hand. He stood there, watching me, his thumb looped in the supple leather of his belt, trying to smooth a smile from his lips. My dress felt tight all of a sudden and fear warred with the pleasure his gaze brought. I didn't want this to turn from dream to nightmare in an instant. I should leave now. But I teased him back. "Well, it should work on nixies and fairies."

What if he were to lunge at me? I wanted him to be a kind man, or at least not a frightening one. The sensations racing up and down my body were at once thrilling and terrifying, yet I yearned for more. It needn't be a lot, just a smile and this talking. I didn't want to know his name. Not knowing made him a stranger. Kept me on my toes. Added to the excitement.

The mage's dusty green tunic creased as he stepped into the meadow, then he eased down to the ground amidst larkspur and chamomile. He leaned back, putting an arm behind him, then toyed with a roughly stitched hem on his tunic with his other hand.

"They say my mother was a nixie. They found me in a basket of reeds, swaddled in seaweed, left on the steps of Cathedral Seil by the mouth of River Remmaz." The mage plucked a chamomile flower, twirled it between his fingers. He mouthed a word over its petals, and it began to glow. "So you claim that kneeling down works even upon me, and so it may. But my question is this: Will it work on you?"

There was space to sit beside him. He'd planned it that way. In a rocky meadow, there was clear space for one person in the center or two people laying side by side.

I knew better than to trust a stranger, but this man, this mage, didn't feel so strange. I knew him. I didn't know how or why; in fact, I was certain I had never met him before. I could never forget those eyes. Not in a lifetime. Not in two. Or a hundred. The emotions they roused within me were unlike anything else. If it weren't for my memory of Judas, I wouldn't have had a moment's hesitance in stepping forward to meet him. Despite the churning in my gut, despite the crude physical exhilaration, I felt relaxed in my soul. At peace.

Then he raised those eyes, and my stomach twisted but it was pleasurable. My skin radiated heat as though I had been sitting too near a fire. Seeing him reclined on the ground—not kneeling, true, but in an even more intimate pose—made me less afraid, yet more shy. I wanted to touch him. To have his cloak brush by me, to let him nudge me to one side of the trail. Something. Anything.

But he wouldn't do it. No, he was upon the ground, getting damp in dewy grass because I had told him to. My skin shivered. I smelled the air for traces of a spell, but found only pollen and the faint decay of a marsh in the center of the glen by the ditch. And there was his own scent—lye soap, horse leather, and wood shavings.

He closed his hand over the chamomile flower. I feared he would crush it, but he mouthed a 'shh' then brought his fist to his lips. Faint words whispered into his fist, then he held his hand out, knuckles down. When he opened his fingers, a cocoon dangled from the chamomile stem. It swayed, then the white petals unspiralled one by one, revealing a yellow moth in the center, its antennae the fuzz of the flower. Its wings were as gossamer and fine as spider's web. It stretched its wings, crawled over his palm and up to his knuckles, then beat its wings. I watched as it lifted and drifted downwind like a dandelion seed.

When I looked back at the mage, his hand was still as he had left it, stretched out towards me, elbow upon bent knee. The chamomile flower was pinched between his two fingers, as normal and natural as though it had just been plucked from the ground. It looked so dainty in his hand knicked from carving. I reached for that hand, then drew back and held my own fingers, uncertain what he would make of the gesture.

"Touch me," he said, making my stomach lurch and pulse quicken. "I assure you I welcome your touch."

Heat flooded through me. I thought I was as hot as I could be, but I was proven wrong: all I needed was to think that he desired my touch, and the world grew hot and began to swim. Still I feared he would grab me, or worse, mock me. Yet his words struck me as true. I reached for him again, feeling dizzy, holding my breath.

My fingernails stroked his knuckle. His breathing froze. I repeated the motion with my fingertip, and he turned his hand over. I felt the soft of his palm. His fingers closed slowly one by one, wrapping about my small finger the way the petals had closed to form the cocoon. He was warm, his hand marked with callouses from ropes. My head spun, all my senses so intense I wanted to pull back but at the same time I needed to know what else I could feel. One look at his closed eyes calmed me, made me confident. I wanted to feel his lips, now parted and moist, but I instead stroked his thumb with my own. It made him smile, and everything else fell away. All there was in the world was that smile and those eyes. The trail and meadow were lost to a dizzy haze and a breeze that tickled my ankles as it brought my dress against my skin.

I wasn't sure if I reached for him or if he lead me, but my hand met his lips. Hot and soft lips on my fingers while my knuckles rubbed cool, prickly stubble of his upper lip. I thought I might wobble. His eyes blazed when they met mine, a fire mindfully contained, frightening and enticing. He blew over my hand, turned it over, and dropped his gaze to my nails. A finger with a newly healed cut traced the lines of my palm, sending thrills through my body. He kissed it. When he pulled away, the wind whisked away moisture left by his lips, giving my palm a second, lingering kiss that made my breath hitch.

When I finally opened my eyes again, he was watching me, eyes not hungry or demanding, but with a question equal parts invitation and challenge. I couldn't breathe, but I didn't want to step away. My knees were weak and getting weaker. I wondered if I'd fall to the ground, but still I remained upright. The dizziness started to fade. I wanted it back. "Kiss me again."

His eyes bolted up to mine, brow furrowed. Angry? Wanting? I couldn't tell. I amended the command. "Please."

The mage's chest swelled with a breath and he kissed my wrist, holding my hand possessively yet lightly. I closed my eyes, willing this moment to continue forever.

"Melody!" A bellow cut through the air, making me jump.

Brother Jacob's yell made me take hold of the mage whose name I did not know. My cheeks burned, feeling ashamed even as I didn't know why. More than that, I felt angry. It had been as a dream, one I hadn't wanted to awaken from.

Ever the hunter, Brother Jacob stood at the edge of the glen, in bushes just off the trail, face pale as though he couldn't believe what he was seeing. Shock faded from Brother Jacob's frame, replaced by a red flush across his cheeks and deep lines as he reached for his bow.

I stepped between my mage and Brother Jacob, though I knew my small frame and Jacob's aim made me a poor shield. However, the mage wouldn't hide behind me. He stood and took hold of my finger.

Brother Jacob's body quivered when the mage spoke. "We are both men who serve the crown. Put up your bow."

Spittle flew from Jacob's lips. "I? I serve the crown? No. I serve the Almighty, the Holy One of the heavens and earth and water." He jabbed his thumb into his own chest with the hand holding his bow. "I serve the spirit. You are a slave to the flesh, seeking desire and pleasure, you are a heathen in the woods."

Brother Jacob did not put up his bow, but neither did he finish notching his arrow, seeming to bear in mind that the mage did serve the king. Brother Jacob jerked his head toward me. "Unhand the girl."

My mage released his hold on my finger and stepped

back. He looked me from head to toe, particularly the bust and hips, the same way Brigid had earlier. "I have not laid hand on her. What is she to you, some fatherless urchin the church took in?"

The muscle in Brother Jacob's jaw jumped. "The girl is in my care. That is all that concerns you."

The mage crossed his arms. "Melody's no girl. She's a woman, though you'll never treat her as one. And she's not yours, but you'll tie her tighter than your hunting boots."

The red in Jacob's cheeks deepened to purple and veins bulged in his neck. "She's a girl still, and better I claim her as my own than to let a scoundrel like you spread your seed in a fertile field only to abandon its care to an honest man."

I knew Jacob was warning me that the mage would forsake me someday, but the rest was lost to me—except to suppose I was the fertile field in question. The mage's jaw clenched.

"The only promises I have made to Melody are those I can keep." He spun on his toe and went to his sweat-soaked horse who had approached us to take a drink from the ditch. The horse's swallows came around heavy pants and flanks quivering to chase off flies. The mage held the horse's reins and motioned to me. "You can come with me if you wish. I travel, but I'll keep you in clothes and you won't starve."

Brother Jacob snorted, closing the distance to me. "A fine prospect. Won't starve! She doesn't need your coins to not starve, witch. I keep her in a house with a good roof and a hot fire. Offer her more than that."

The mage swung onto his horse, his saddle creaking, a new purchase or gift, further support that he was recently marked. "At present I cannot. Not while I search for real witches and warlocks, my dear monk." The mage nodded to me. "Would you come to aid me, or do you seek to remain?"

Brother Jacob pointed his bow at the man on the horse. "That's enough from you."

"I would hear it from Melody." The mage met my gaze.

Brother Jacob shook my shoulder. "Don't look him in the eyes. You never know when they're channelling the Dark One."

Fire bolted through me and I yanked my arm away. "I know when a spell is cast, Brother Jacob."

Brother Jacob shook his head, but the mage looked at me in a new light. Brother Jacob crossed his arms. "Then do tell me your thoughts on this matter, girl."

Embarrassed, I looked up the mage and admitted, "I do not know you."

The mage's lips pursed. "I said I would earn your name, and so you would earn mine. Still, I think you know me even without an introduction. If you are concerned, you may leave me at any time, should you so wish it. I know people who would provide work."

I hesitated. I might have been tempted to go—I probably would have gone—but Brother Jacob was here, reminding me that life was no dream. It demanded caution and planning. "I really couldn't."

"Could not or will not?"

I drew lines in the ground, bending grass blades under

the toe of my boot. "I will not."

The brothers were a certain truth—they would keep me well and I knew what to expect. This mage was a stranger, a delusion, a trick of my fancy. I couldn't trust him.

"As you would have it." The mage's voice was tense and had lost its rhythmic quality. It made my throat lock and my stomach plummet. "Though your guardian would paint me otherwise, I will not have a woman who does not wish to first have me. Farewell, Melody, it was a pleasure to meet you."

He nodded to Brother Jacob, who was gripping his bow with white knuckles. The mage didn't look at me as he clucked his horse onto the path and started down the road, his shoulders stiff. Relief and regret washed over me at once, as though I had been both wise and incredibly foolish. I wanted to charge down the road and call for the man to stop, to tell me his name, and to take me with him —but the words wouldn't move past the block in my throat.

Brother Jacob snared my arm in the same hand as his arrow, the fletching becoming marred when it rubbed against my sleeve with every step as we walked some ways up the trail. I pried his fingers off my arm. "That hurts."

"Not as bad as if he had gotten what he wanted from you." Brother Jacob rammed his arrow back into the quiver, watching the trees as though worried the mage would come back.

I bit my lip to keep back a scream. "He merely kissed my hand."

"That's how it starts."

"How what starts?" When Jacob did not answer, I began to pace, kicking at sticks as they entered my path. "You tell me to not sin, the books say 'not to engage in carnal acts' but what are those? No one tells me anything."

Brother Jacob resumed shaking. "I can't tell you. No one can. To even know of their existence makes a person weak." He opened his fists. "I know. I was not always a monk, Melody, I was a warrior until the nightmares started. This is my cure. I devote myself to a pure life. I've done things other men would sicken to hear of. I've done them to men and women alike. When I took the cowl, I received a new life and a new name, but nothing can make me forget the transgressions I made at your age. No, you are better to know nothing at all and remain a child forever than to have even a scent of the filthy desire that plagues humankind every hour of every day."

My mind reeled with so much new information. What was Brother Jacob saying? It was too much to comprehend all at once. I grasped onto the least shocking thing I could. "Certainly it is not so often!"

He swallowed hard and his face darkened with heavy lines and sad eyes. "Very much so. It is more of a taunt the more you know of it, and no matter how long or how hard you try, you can never forget the sick pleasure and twisted desires. This is why it is best that you not know. This is why you should remain a girl. Forget about womanhood. Your work is important, you are holy. Stay that way."

Today I seemed to spend more time dizzy than sane. I

leaned against a boulder. "But why would the Holy One make pleasure if it wasn't meant to be enjoyed?"

"He didn't. The Dark One made pleasure as a temptation. Stay pure. It is the salvation for us all."

I couldn't believe that the joy of being with the mage was something that came from the Dark One. I wouldn't believe it. "How am I to stay pure if no one tells me what to avoid?"

"Avoid it all. Let no man touch you. Don't even look at a boy. When you bring a unicorn to Easter, there are so many souls who come to us, who turn to the Holy One for the first time in their lives, or who come back to us after falling to temptation. Do this, Melody, and think of all the people you save. Think of all the girls who do not die at the claws of a dragon."

I swallowed, remembering dragons. How many would kill a girl if they could? Did they ever intent to kill the virgin they received? Then again, was my selfish pleasure worth even one death? Heart sinking, I stared out in the direction the mage had gone, envisioning the creek he was probably crossing now. "You're right, Brother Jacob."

The strain went out from his frame. He bowed his head and offered a prayer of thanks. Then he said, "Speak the good words with me, Melody. And promise me you'll never again leave the cottage without permission."

My throat locked. I didn't promise, but when he started a prayer, I joined in with him, even as my thoughts wandered to the stranger on the horse who I knew I'd known long before I'd started memories from this life. I wished I could tell him I was sorry.

CHAPTER 11

This year, I didn't wait for Brother Jacob to ask if I was pure for the Easter hunt. I had instead gathered up my items, locked eyes with him at the door, and told him, "It's time to hunt. Come or be left behind."

I was in no mood for opposition, and nor was I in a mood to be delayed. I had to get out of that cottage, before I pulled out Brigid's hair or threw one of Brother Adams' books on the fire. What had happened to the peace and family that we once had, I didn't know. That place rubbed and hurt like a boot that was too small for the foot.

Years had passed. The first one went by quietly enough. A hunt. Holiday festivities I tried to avoid, as usual. A long, cold winter that killed many livestock and lead to us housing a cow and four goats in our already cramped cottage. I accepted this better than Brigid did, but when winter gave way to summer and Brother Adams imposed stricter rules on where we could go and for how long, I knew there was something else happening. Brigid ranted for hours at a time while we picked berries within view of the cottage that autumn, and I didn't tell her that this was my fault. Brother Jacob hadn't told anyone else about the mage who had kissed me, a man I secretly watched the roads for.

The second year I went to two separate dragons. One posed no threat to me in particular, simply wanted to have the bragging rights of having cajoled a virgin sacrifice out of the villagers. She kept me for a few months then went into hibernation. The second dragon was the brother of that one, and refused to be outdone, so he kept me in his dragonhaunt for half the year.

It was nearly the third year when I returned to the cottage. Having spent so much time on my own, I resented the rules laid in place to keep me in line. Brigid frequently told me, "You haven't been here, you don't know what it's like." She refused to say much else on any topic. Her bread making had improved. When I said this, she took it as an insult, "Wasn't good enough for you before, was it?" I stopped trying to get her to speak with me after that. Once, I heard the two brothers argue outside, but I couldn't tell what about, only hear their tones. The closer to spring it became, the worse it got.

Mealtime conversations had become tense, if they happened at all. Brother Adams took my silence as a sign that I needed more prayers, and I took the increased lessons with annoyance at best and an argument at the worst. All ended with both of us confined to separate dark rooms doing penance. Brother Jacob halted three yelling matches by grabbing my cloak, tossing it over my shoulders, and taking me for a walk which ended only when the arches of my feet ached to the point of hobbling my gait. Quieter debates Brigid put a stop to with the suggestion of some chore or another which parted me and Brother Adams. I had done my best to forget the mage, he was only a man, a stranger who probably did not have my best interests in mind, but I couldn't forgive the brothers for adding more rules since the brief encounter with the mage.

Now, Brother Jacob appeared in the door, the morning light touching his face and revealing thinning hair which had not yet been combed. He called out, "You once told me not to hunt with hate in my heart."

I paused, my basket digging into the flesh of my arm. White hair covered Brother Jacob's bare chest, and I belatedly remembered washing both his tunics after he had made them stink from working in the garden and mending a fence. Wearing only his trousers, he wouldn't come after me. Not immediately, anyway. From the safety of my clothed state, I felt emboldened enough to say, "It isn't hate. I'm angry. At you!"

To my surprise, Brother Jacob stepped off the door threshold, walked over prickly pine needles barefoot, and came to a stop before me. "It's Adams who wants Brigid leashed. The same rules apply to you so there's no mutiny."

"I don't care about the rules." I found that I really didn't. The rules didn't help matters, if anything they aggravated me and brought the real anger to the surface. "I'm angry about the mage."

Someone else would have had to think about what I meant, or at least take a few seconds to remember. Not Brother Jacob. He knew who I was speaking about, and that told me that the event had been burned into his memory as well as mine. An annoyed sigh crossed his lips, then that fell away to a stern expression. "I kept you safe. I'm not going to apologize."

I didn't answer. I knew he wouldn't apologize, and I didn't want him to. He'd done as he thought he should. Just that simple. But the knowledge didn't shake my slow-burning fury that had taken years to build.

He put a hand on his hip and asked, "It was a long time ago, Melody. What was so important about him? He's gone. We can't undo the past. What more do you want?"

"To go with him." The words appeared in the air between us. I didn't even feel them pass my lips. I didn't even think the words. They just happened, but once they were said, I knew they were true. But it had been a long time ago, and I had no way of knowing if the offer to go still stood, or if the mage was alive or even where he was. Tears stung my eyes and I looked away, but not before Brother Jacob rubbed his brow. The wind blew between us, stirring a bit of snow off a drift which was taking its time dying beneath the spring sun.

"Melody," he said at last. In that one word, I heard the pain and sympathy and frustration. "You didn't know him. Why was he so important to you?"

"I don't know," I said, breathing hard. The last time my chest had felt so tight was my first day in the big church.

Brother Jacob stepped closer, but didn't reach out to me. He crossed his arms and looked up into the sky. "Amazing how fast it happens."

"How fast what happens?"

His eyes darted down to mine, and I thought he saw me for once as something other than a child. "How fast you can lose your heart."

My breathing froze and I squeezed my eyes shut.

"It'll come back. Give it time."

But it has been time. It has been a long time. I bit my lip so hard I tasted blood. At last, I shook out the words, "Is it ever the same?"

"It's sadder, stronger, and more beautiful than ever," Brother Jacob said, his voice thick and husky. "We say that we lose them, but that isn't true. We lose the bit of our heart that they take with them."

I didn't think that was any more of a comfort than actually losing the person, but it did explain the ache in my chest. Brother Jacob motioned to the road. "I'll make my preparations. Go for now. In three days, I'll meet you by the milestone at The Forks."

If I hugged him, I'd start to cry, and I didn't want that, so I instead flung myself down a trail my feet knew well, running as hard as I could to get away before my tears burst and I slipped to the ground. Three days, he'd said. Three days for me to be out in the woods alone and free. To go anywhere I wished. It was better than an apology.

I spent those days not wandering like I thought I would, but making camp by a creek. No pots to clean. No meals to make. No bibles or songs or house rules to obey. The freedom unwound the constriction around my chest, and by the end of the third day, I felt older and ready for the unicorn hunt. But a thread of melancholy had been woven into my being now, and I knew that nothing could

ever be the same as before I'd met the dragons. Before I'd
met the mage.

At the start of the third day, I set out for the place
where the main road split into four directions, and waited
in a tree until I saw the hunched shape of Brother Jacob
in a cowl. He stopped and looked up at me. I shimmied
down the tree. He pointed to the hunting grounds for
this year, and I went in that direction.

Days slid by as I strolled through the forest, my hair
about my elbows, flying into my face with every twist of
the wind which rustled dry grasses and made tree limbs
creak and moan. Clear springs and snow drops formed a
scattered path, one I knew well after so many years of
hunting. Doing this was more peaceful and healing than
anything else could have been. Staying in the cottage had
been doing nothing more than rubbing a wound, making
it swell and fester. Out here I could breathe. Out here, I
knew I had to use all my senses to find the unicorn's
favorite places. It gave me something to focus on and
accomplish.

I studied my reflection in a clear pool when I knelt
down to wait for a unicorn. Though I saw no beauty in
my round cheeks and unruly hair, I saw no hideousness in
my body, unless a curved belly and healthy skin was to be
considered ugly. As I listened to the trembles of a hare
and the gurgle of a spring, I heard also the whispers of
accusation in my soul.

Words from a dragon came back to me. "You are no
longer a babe, yet you keep yourself not, but take food
from your benefactors, wear the clothes they give you, in

return for an obedience you only feign."

A year ago I would have called him a liar. Two years ago, I would have dubbed him the Devil. Three years ago, I would have shaken my head in pity for his ignorance.

But I had said nothing. Now, as I saw myself in the water, I could only notice that the hymns had faded from my lips some time ago, and I could only bow my head in disgrace and say, "I know."

Slowly, a white head appeared over my shoulders, dark eyes concealed beneath thick white locks. Breath burst on the back of my neck, hot at first, then cold when the air took away the heat. A spiralled horn the length of my arm bobbed overhead.

I jumped.

The unicorn was unalarmed by my reaction, and regarded me with brown eyes which caught the glowing moonlight off the spring and reflected it back. It snuffled again, smelled my hair. A long, dexterous tongue slipped out of its mouth and it wrapped around a brunette curl and drew it into its lips, chewing.

Not able to resist a smile, I slowly reached up and pulled my hair back before it could try to swallow.

The horn bumped my ear as it lowered its head to look me in the eye. Unlike other animals smelling of dust and sweat and feces, unicorns smelled as roses do after a rain, sweet and clear and potent.

I casually glanced at the shelter of boughs Brother Jacob was concealed beneath. There came no shifting of leaves as he notched an arrow. There was no noise coming from him at all, which was unusual...unless he happened to be asleep? The idea was startling, he was always so good about remaining awake, but it was the only thing that could explain his lack of movement.

"It is the two of us, then," I whispered to the beast.

He blinked his eye, long white lashes brushing my cheek and flicking away a tear. He raised his head, to smell my breath. I blew softly into his nose and said, "I was thinking of leaving once this is over. Have you come to kill me for that?"

The unicorn pulled back, shook his head, the horn darting from side to side before my face for a second, his mane like a horse's, flying in loose, thick lock as as fine as any human's hair.

He raised his lips to my nose again, inhaling deeply of my breath, then turned to lick my cheek. Hot, wet, and a delightful mixture of rough texture and soft dexterity, his tongue cleaned first one cheek, then the other.

Much the same as one can not help but smile at the kitten who kneads its claws into flesh, I could not but smile and close my eyes to the caress of the unicorn. I tried to not laugh as it stepped back and bobbed its head while flicking its tongue in and out of each nostril.

Snores reached me from Brother Jacob's position.

I reached up and touched the horn. It was smooth and warm beneath my fingers. I whispered, "I won't kill you."

But would he kill me?

His ears pricked forward and his head twisted. I lifted my own head and stared in the direction the unicorn was, but all I saw was a blur of white as another body lunged through the air, black hooves cresting the tops of snow drops, horn flashing in the moonlight.

The first unicorn jumped away, but not fast enough. The horn of the second unicorn plunged into its neck and ripped back out.

Racing backward on all fours, I tried to put distance between us, but I was no where near as fast as the unicorns, and soon the other unicorn turned to face me.

Two blue eyes seared into my skull.

Its ears twitched towards me, and its flank quivered. It stepped forward. Then it lowered its horn. Setting my jaw, I refused to bow down, and I refused to be pushed to the side. Taking a deep breath of my scent, the unicorn's nostrils flared wide and his chest inflated. His upper lip curled back over his nose, smelling me. Then he bobbed his head and nickered, similar to a horse's noise, but with less volume and a higher pitch. He advanced, thick lips tugging on my dress even as his horn disturbed my cloak.

Though I had thought the forest still before, now it was even more so, not even the creek flowing from the pool making any noise of comfort. Brambles around the clearing now seemed thicker, even the rabbit trails disappearing from view. No birds were in the trees, nor squirrels, everything hiding in their nests as the unicorn took yet another step forward.

My back touched tree trunk.

Now I recognized the pitch of the silence, the entrapment surrounding me. On the air, I tasted the ashy flavor of a spell. Whatever this magic was, it was not good. My dress ripped, leaving the bare skin of my hip bone open to winter's kiss.

When the unicorn's tongue scraped over my skin, I slapped his nose. He jerked back, and I bolted for the brambles. An angry cry pierced the air, and hooves followed.

Branches stung me, but they stung the pursuing unicorn harder. He gained on me, and I ducked head over heels down a hill, following a trail too steep and too narrow for the great beast. Trumpeting again, he ran to find another way down. Though the cloak had cushioned me from a terrible blow, my back had collided with at least two sharp rocks, and my hunched-over running was a slow jog.

Only when my feet hit a road trenched with merchant's carts did I slow my pace. Light shined through barren tree limbs, and I felt certain the unicorn would not follow me. Aching with every step, I examined my basket. Broken from my tumble, it was missing a few items, but I was rather surprised to find I still had it at all. I rescued the fire dragon's scale from falling out, and realized my knife was gone, as were the berries I had picked.

What was that thing? It was unlike any unicorn I had ever encountered before. They were scared by the slightest sneeze, and they were certainly much smaller than that beast.

That thing, that king of the forest, knew how to manipulate magic. It had sent power out through the nearby forest, acting on whatever was living out there. A monster like that would easily have coaxed a weary man to sleep.

But if the large unicorn had made Jacob sleep, then what had it wanted with me? I shivered to think what that might be. Where would I best meet up with Brother

Jacob again? The Forks, possibly. But if he couldn't come, or couldn't come in time, I needed to go where there were other people. A village, perhaps.

Every bend, I found myself watching over my shoulder in a way that I had never done in my life. It wanted me, I grew more certain of that with each passing second, but I could not think of why.

A few bends later, the sunlight was gone, and I again smelled a storm in the sky. The birds whispered to one another. It would snow to cover wolf dens. The trees groaned. It was going to freeze their bark. I followed the road through darkening air, first seeing the outline of a church in a valley, then smelling the brook which went around the town. Stopping and leaning against a tree, I stared out at the one path which went to the town, and I saw it there.

The unicorn was guarding the bridge, waiting for me.

Despite the aches in my feet, legs, and back, I pushed off from the tree and retreated back into the woods. At least I recognized the town now, known by humans as Weaverham, but known by its dragon as Lanolin. He said it was what it smelled like: Sheep oil.

"Melody!"

My heart skipped; that was Brother Jacob. I ran out from behind the trees, into the road where Brother Jacob rode one horse and lead another. "I'm here!"

"Melody." Brother Jacob breathed my name and his shoulders relaxed. The horses stepped forward, nickering, but one squealed when The Mule bit his haunches and pushed his way to the front. He buried his head in my chest and glared at the horses while I scratched the knot on top of his head, his mane moist with sweat.

"Melody, I couldn't find you. What happened? Was there a wolf?"

My brow furrowed. "Wolf?"

"There was so much blood, I...I wasn't sure if you were alive." Brother Jacob swung off his horse and stood beside me. He reached out and touched my shoulder, as though to convince himself he wasn't seeing a specter.

"Didn't you see the body of the unicorn? Two of them got into a fight over me."

Brother Jacob shook his head. "Never has it happened before. It isn't in their nature. You must be mistaken."

I lowered my eyes and scratched The Mule's ears. Brother Jacob sighed. He said, "I believe what you saw, but whatever that thing was, it was not a Divine One. Come, hurry on the horse. The hunt is off. We're taking you home."

I pushed The Mule aside and mounted. After meeting that monster in the forest, and knowing that he was still out there somewhere looking for me, I didn't feel like finishing the hunt, either. I couldn't help but to wonder if Anna had really been impure...or if, perhaps she had simply been too wise for it.

When we reached the cottage, I tended to the animals while Brother Jacob relayed all that had happened to Brother Adams. Brother Adams shook his head. "There will be no unicorn this year, then. The village will not be pleased."

"She is fortunate to have survived at all, and you think

of the villagers!" Brother Jacob's voice was venom, and it made Brother Adams lift a brow. Hearing him defend me made my cheeks warm. Adams laid his hand over Jacob's shoulder.

"I am as glad as you to not have the heavy burden of burying another daughter of the Holy One, but we must be reasonable. The villagers will want to know why Melody hasn't brought back a unicorn this year. There will be talk. More so than the other rumors."

"What other rumors?" I asked, but Brother Adams pursed his lips.

Brother Jacob shook his head, a way to tell me to let this topic drop. It wasn't as urgent as the main concern, so I didn't press. Brother Jacob sighed. "What are we going to tell them?"

"We should speak the truth," I said, hanging the bridles off my shoulders and arranging the tack on my body with particular care so I wouldn't miss out on eavesdropping.

Brother Adams' eyes lit ablaze. "That is the last thing we should say. We will say the unicorn was frightened when Melody sneezed."

"What?" Insult blazed through me. I looked to Brother Jacob, who had closed his eyes and let out a slow breath.

He said, "That will be what we say. You won't speak of anything else."

"But they'll think it an excuse—they'll think I'm impure."

"And what would they think if they heard the truth?" Brother Jacob rubbed his eyes as though they ached.

"I—" The words stuck in my throat as I realized what

he meant. Fatigue crashed in around me. I whispered, "They'd think I was a witch."

"And so we won't speak of it."

Suddenly the saddle blanket and bridles felt heavy. I nodded, and said, "Very well. But I want to speak with Brigid about it. She'll understand."

A line appeared over Brother Adams' brow and his face turned red. He said tensely, "You cannot see her. She is ill."

What had him angry? Being ill was nothing to be upset over. My heart quickened, to think that I might lose Brigid after the chilly way our interactions had been lately.

"Then I'll go to her right away," I said, hastening towards the cottage.

"She isn't there," Brother Adams called after me. I paused, turned around, and saw Brother Jacob mouth a prayer. Brother Adams met his gaze and continued, "She is with a healer. Brigid is not to be seen, by anyone. It is the devil tempting her."

Certainly if there was anyone who could help her, particularly on this issue, it would be me. What possible reason could they have for isolating her? "But, I'm as close as she has to a sister, surely I—"

"No," said Brother Adams.

Why couldn't I see her? Brigid was all I had here. We'd grown into women together. We understood challenges and things that no one else could, because no one else had been in our occupation. My chest swelled, tight in my dress. She knew me in a way that the brothers could not. She knew me in a way that my own flesh and blood could not. She knew what I'd seen, what my conflicts were, everything.

I looked to Brother Jacob, who said, "Melody, listen to Brother Adams. You are tired, as am I, and the two of us will need your help in making a pilgrimage. The villagers will want us to lead them to the monastery."

"Of course," I said, glad for something to focus on but still stinging from the rejection of my help. If I knew where Brigid had gone, I would have gone after her, but I couldn't think of a single place where Brother Adams would send her. He had said she was with the healer, but if she was in isolation there, then my odds of finding her were struck to nill. Of course, I might be able to find her but...only if Brigid wanted me to. She would have left a clue in the cottage for me. Head bowed, I said, "I will make our preparations."

"Melody," said Brother Adams, making me stop again. "It will be Jacob and me who go. You will spend this Easter alone, to meditate on the message you have been given."

Was I to be punished for that monster's advances? Without Brigid or anyone to speak with?

"But..." I stopped, seeing Brother Jacob's grim expression. I realized he agreed with Brother Adams. Suddenly, it dawned on me: Brigid was gone, and with her all of the house rules and supervision. It had been her they had been watching, after all, and not me. For some reason the knowledge didn't make breathing any easier. Looking down at the blankets coated in horse hair in my arms, I said, "I will use the time wisely."

The time until they left passed quickly. Despite myself,

I spent most of that time looking for a message that Brigid might have left. Eventually, I did find a note wedged into Brigid's favorite passage. It read, *I have gone where you should not follow. I say this because I love you. Brigid.*

Tears of betrayal welled in my eyes, things I tried to keep hidden while the brothers finished packing their rolls of clothing and tying it down to a horse. I straggled after them, watching from the threshold while the two men steadied horses—one which was theirs, another which was borrowed from a farmer. As Brother Adams mounted his horse, he told me to stay inside. I did not respond, but looked to Brother Jacob, who nodded, understanding that I would wander the woods as I saw fit, and he would find me when they returned.

If I was to find solace in this time of reflection, I found none as I walked the grounds around the cottage, refusing to be frightened by man or beast. Day found me restless, and nights were sleepless.

I dreamed of a hunt that night. I was walking in the forest, pulling twigs from my hair, fighting with branches and tripping over roots. I fell into a tangle of berry bushes, their thorns piercing my skin and sinking into my flesh, digging deeper when I struggled.

Then I felt warm breath bursting on the back of my neck, and turned to find a unicorn leaning over me. He blinked his eye, long white lashes brushing my cheek and flicking away a tear. His tongue cleaned first one cheek, then the other. Wherever he touched was healed, the bleeding stopping and wound closing.

The berry bushes around me grew blossoms, red instead of white, and far larger than they should be.

When I next looked, the leaves had changed, and I was lying in a bed of roses.

I angled my head back and felt soft lips arch down my skin. Through thick lashes, I saw a head of dark hair and green eyes that glowed in the night, his skin blending in with the shadows while my skin stood out like a white petal in the night. The man's cheeks were rough beneath my fingertips, and in that instant, happiness sung though my body and beyond. It was so, so good to see him again. When I tried to tell him that, he smiled and covered my mouth with his. Talking was the last thing on my mind after that. It seemed for ages and eternity that imaginary kisses trailed down my neck.

And then the dream faded into morning. I rubbed my eyes in the bright light, realizing I had slept through half the day, still feeling too hot, still feeling the confused dizziness from before. With the realization that I was in the cottage, alone, came a sinking sensation that made me wish I could fall though the bed back into the dream, or that I would hear the steady footfalls of the mage coming to the door with a pail of creek water. I laid in bed for many minutes, too terrified to get up and realize that I was truly alone. Time continued on, and my bruised heart accepted that the mage had been gone long ago. But what of the rest? The kisses had felt so real, same with the caresses and the love.

Dream merged with reality in my waking state, and I wondered: Had that been how it happened? Or had it been different? Slowly, I crossed to the table with a pitcher of cold water. Splashing it onto my face, I grew more confused as I tried to separate dream memories from real memories. The unicorn, the man, the bed of roses, all of it seemed likely to be real, but I knew that one was fact, and the other was a dream. Which was which? I couldn't remember what was memory and what was a fabrication of the night. Some people said that dreams were real, that they were harbingers of the future, or messages about what course of action was needed. Was this one of those dreams? I'd never been prone to restless nights, or dreams which I could recall so vividly in the morning. Was this a message? I needed to find out.

I knew I wanted to find the mage and go with him. But it was impossible. Even considering that he was somewhere in the kingdom, the kingdom was a large place, and at any given time he might be on the opposite end, or one of us might inadvertently be following the other. This was even thinking that he would welcome me back, or that he hadn't already found a woman to marry. Or that he wasn't dead. And that he was actually a decent person to be with. There were so many reasons that I *shouldn't* go and no solid reason to encourage me to take to the road.

I walked around where a fire hadn't been lit in the hearth for days, everything put away and in order so meticulous that it looked like no one lived there. I had hoped Brother Jacob would be back. I felt the need to talk to someone, but who else could I speak with? I didn't know where Brigid was, or even if she wanted to see me. I couldn't confide in anyone else. Who would hear me through and not proclaim me a witch?

A few people who could help me came to mind, but nearly all of them would be going on the Easter

Pilgrimage. All but one. She was a woman who claimed no ability to prophesize, but believed in them anyway. I didn't know what to make of this dream. My head and heart seemed to be telling me different things, a circumstance which I was accustomed to, but this was the first time in a long time that I thought it would be wrong to follow my heart. There had always been support for it in the past.

As quickly as I wondered this, I knew the answer.

I needed help to sort this out. Before the brothers arrived back home. Before that thing in the woods realized I'd left grounds sanctified against anything evil. I restocked the food in my basket, then flew outside, striding across the pasture with purpose. With all the others gone and Ragnark's tooth about my neck for protection, I took only what I needed to survive, and I left the cottage. The Mule raised his head, and followed me.

CHAPTER 12

Moonlight cloaked my shoulders, the curve of my hip, the muscles on my abdomen as I swam in the shallows of the lake outside my old village. My bracelet made from chips of unicorn horn purified the water as I cut through it. At last tired, if nothing else, I sat on a rock by the water and combed my hair, watching the night about me, watching owls fly soundlessly over the meadow.

My reflection caught my gaze, and I was surprised by the stranger staring back at me. Though the form and shape of myself was there, I saw something else in the way the water rippled, making my eyes seem to wink like stars behind clouds. I saw power. It hadn't been there before. I stared at those eyes for a long time, unsure what to do with them. The Mule sauntered over to me and started to rub his face over my back, sending me sprawling over wet rocks slick with moss and coating my skin in itchy hair.

I splashed water at The Mule, which made him shake his head, lick his lips, and then take a drink next to my thigh. Old as he was now, mostly bones and ragged hair, he nevertheless had walked with me every day. We stayed off the main roads, taking game trails, drinking from fresh water and sleeping under the boughs of weeping willows. In four days, we had cut through the thickest parts of the forest, a shortcut I wouldn't have even thought about taking less than two years ago. Sticky and sore, I had made camp by the lake and cleaned up. It wouldn't do to look like we had wandered through the forest.

I dried in the cool of the night while grooming The Mule, not minding the hair and dust that came off his coat. In the end, he looked like a respectable animal, no matter how old. He kept watch over the shoreline as I bathed a second time, this time scrubbing harder to rid myself of his oil. When exhaustion set in, I fell asleep beneath his belly as he stood guard over me, something we had started to do following Ragnark's death.

Morning came with bluebird songs and a hurried breakfast, then we walked the final stretch of our journey, a nervous knot tying up my gut. As the light beat down on the earth, we stepped out of the wilds and into meadows cropped close by flocks of ewes with black lambs.

In the center of the field, sitting upon a blanket and wrestling with stitching her leather boots, was a girl with brown curls and a round face. Had I not known otherwise, I would have thought that she was one of my sisters, or that we had been transported back in time and I was looking down at myself days before Noble had come. She looked up, startled, when The Mule stamped his feet at flies. Her hands went instantly to the shepherd's crook.

"Go away."

From this angle, I could see her features better. She looked like my second-eldest sister, but with light brown eyes and a heart-shaped mouth. I couldn't resist a smile at her. "Are your grandparents still living?"

It stung me when I realized that they might not be. In my mind, they hadn't aged from when I left. I hadn't been prepared for the thought that one or both of them were dead, or that something had happened to the place which had always been permanent in my mind. Suddenly, I didn't know if this was such a good idea, after all. Was I ready to hear and see how time had treated them?

The girl's lips opened and she shut them, then reconsidered and said, "They don't know you. Go away."

Remembering when I had said those same words, I smiled. "Do they still live in the house in the valley, or has your mother taken up residence there?"

The girl's face went white. "How do you know?"

Had I been thinking a little more, I would have realized that it would frighten her to have a strange woman walk out of the woods where there wasn't so much as a trail, then ask in detail about the residents of her home. The abbot's words about others being scared of my mind rang back to me. When The Mule nudged me, I scratched the poll of his head, gaining dusty grease beneath nails I'd tried so hard the night before to clean.

"I'm your Aunt Melody." That was an odd thought, to walk home one day and find out I was an aunt. I'd always expected that my sisters would have children by now, but I wasn't expecting my niece to be so old. "You look like you are about nine years old?"

"Ten," she said, insulted. I remembered when I had been eager to grow old.

I rubbed The Mule's ears, thinking that a bit of blood from the ear mites wouldn't matter now that I'd soiled my fingers. "I was nine when I first met him."

I wondered how long ago that had been. Ten years ago at least, likely more. That put me in my early twenties. It was a dizzying thought. I began to walk towards the valley.

"Wait! You can't just walk in unannounced! You're trespassing," the girl called, running in front of me and standing there, hands on hips.

What she thought she could do to stop me, I would have liked to know, but didn't want to taunt her. I laughed. "You can come with me if you wish."

She did, but only to tell me the entire way about why I shouldn't go. She was still telling me while we rounded the corner of a shed, and I caught sight of a tiny hovel, a round thing of mud and wattle with a weak trickle of smoke coming out the top. "...Grandfather has a dog, a mean one, you..."

"Melody, you go back to the flock right now!" A voice yelled from the house, then a woman with a stooped back and white hair stepped into the sun, and her eyes opened in shock. "Melody?"

"Mother," I said, then the words stuck in my throat. I didn't know what to say. Neither did she, though she threw down a crook she used like a cane and ran to me. When my hands wrapped around her shoulders, I was surprised by how small she had become.

She held my face in her hands, studying my face

frantically, as though fearing that something terrible must have brought me to her doorstep. "Child, whatever has you here? You aren't supposed to return. But come, come inside and have drink. Melody, put Melody's mule in a pen by itself and give it water."

I wasn't sure what to say at first. Encountering my niece Melody had made me feel odd but still an adult, but coming face to face with my mother made me feel small again. All the reasoning skills I'd learned from the tutors disappeared into a wisp of smoke, and there I was, exactly in the same frame of mind as I had been when I left the first time. I blurted, "I need help, Mother. I don't know what to do."

Her eyes, lined with wrinkles and drooping, were still bright and clear as they studied me. Gray streaks marked her hair, thick strands which were replacing the finer, darker hair of her youth. But she was still there, in the way she held her shoulders, even if her feet shuffled a little as she walked. Mother said, "Come inside daughter, and tell me what you will."

Inside, the rows of beds I remembered from childhood were gone, replaced with a bench to sit upon near the fire and a chair padded with pillows flattened from use. All but a few of the clay pots from my childhood were gone, likely broken and discarded, and the armfuls of sewing to be done was now nothing but my father's tunic in a chair with a bone needle half-finished stitching a tear. My sisters were gone, now, leaving only my parents and the traces of a few young children. It was a stranger's home now, even though I was welcome in it.

Mother poured me ale into a wooden cup, and sat

down beside me. Though I might have startled her with my outburst earlier, we didn't talk about it, not yet. I had so many questions that came to mind, questions I hadn't known I would want answered until I found myself here. We spoke for a time of my siblings and father. My father was with Melody's parents in one of the pastures, tending to lambs. Six of my sisters had died, three as children, one from illness, and two during childbirth. The others were married, the eldest still to her blacksmith, one to a neighboring farmer—this was the girl's father— one to a merchant, one to another shepherd, another to a weaver, and the youngest to a soldier.

When I was first going to Ragnark, I had felt sad to miss my sister's wedding. Now I realized I'd missed all of their weddings, so many funerals, and more than that, also their children's births and infant deaths. It was as though I had been the one who had died, and now was returning, to find that life had passed me by.

"But enough of us," Mother said. "Tell me what has brought you here."

I told her everything, starting with Ragnark and ending with meeting my niece. At first it was hard to make my lips move, but soon I gained strength and the story told itself. Mother didn't gasp or cry. She would nod when I paused or at times refilled my cup to moisten my throat. When I was finished, my lips were cracked and I felt as though someone had pulled my spine out of my back. Rubbing my eyes the way Brother Jacobs did, I slouched back into a chair and admitted, "And that's that. I don't know what's coming, but...I think it's time for a change. Just don't know how."

Mother's lips, though thinner, curved into the same smile as I remembered. She said, "I never told you what happened to me while I was pregnant with you. A walnut-skinned woman who had stopped by the house begging for food laid hand on my belly and she told me, 'Forget that I have asked you for bread. Give me only water. The child in you will be unlike any of the others. Let her be what she will. Let her grow and walk the world freely. She will be your delight, and this will only make your duties harder, but she knows what she must do. Support her in this.' And so we have. When you first became aware of the world, you wanted so much to go out into it. We resisted it for a time, but when they needed a girl to go to the dragon...we knew it had to be you, even before you heard and took the idea into your own head."

What was I to make of that tale? She had indeed never breathed a word of it to me before, but I did remember hearing an occasional grumble which this was explained by. I tried to smile, but couldn't. The prophesy was a mixed blessing, and it in no way helped me to see what it was that I should do now. Other than perhaps to trust myself, which I was less than inclined to do. Trust was one thing. Doing something stupid was an entirely different matter. I sighed. "Mother...I can't abandon my post. They count on me."

Mother took my hand in hers. It was drier than I remembered, like parchment, and her bones were light in my palm. Nevertheless it was a bad idea to think her fragile, this woman with garden dirt under her nails and the glint of steel in her eyes. "I won't tell you what to do because I don't know. But you do. You alone know what you need to do."

"But I don't know."

"Then you aren't asking yourself deep enough," Mother said. She gave my hand a squeeze. "You can stay here until you are ready to move on again."

Father came that night, and I spoke with him in words that hummed through the air, and I knew for certain the reason that his sheep were the strongest and the healthiest. It was the same reason that farmers brought their lamed horses to him, and the same reason that others asked him for help in training dogs.

He knew the secrets of animals the way I knew the secrets behind songs and stories. Father never could have passed the king's tests to be a mage, but what he had was a gift that blessed the village and by extension the whole kingdom.

There was something peaceful about him, and it was this power that Noble must have seen on the day he had visited them. It was a gift I saw in myself, a tending gift, but I didn't know what it was I was meant to tend. Father once laid hands on The Mule and said he was old, but strong, and his gaze had met mine. He never said it was due to me The Mule was so old and so strong, but it passed between us anyway.

I stayed with them for a week, keeping the house clean, helping on occasion with the sheep, receiving visits from this or that sister. On the seventh morning, I was fetching water from the well when I saw a familiar horse and rider walk the muddy path to my parent's house.

I met him on the doorstep as he said to my mother, "...

we don't know where she has gone, I'm sorry to say this."

"She came here," Mother said, nodding to me.

Noble turned around. "Melody!" His face registered shock, then relief. Noble, who had escorted me across so many roads, had nothing to say.

Mother said to me, "Every year after Easter, he pays us a visit and tells us about you."

I nodded, and brought the water inside. I sat down on the bench, closed my eyes, and took a slow breath while the two murmured outside. Father had told me the night before that I needed to find whatever it was that I was called to tend, then I needed to tend it until my days were over. The king needed us as badly as he needed those who harvested wheat and lead the troops, but we couldn't work unless we had found the thing we needed to tend. But what was that?

My eyes drifted over the smoky rafters filled with dried herbs and hanging lamb. I pursed my lips. In a rush, I grabbed my basket and flew out the door.

Noble was mounting his horse when I appeared beside him astride The Mule. I waved farewell to my mother, my father, and to Melody, then nudged The Mule down the road. Noble raised a surprised brow at me but said nothing, letting the slow beats of our animals fill the void of questions he didn't dare ask, and I wouldn't have known how to answer.

When we rounded a bend by an ancient weeping willow, Noble asked me, "Will you be returning to your post, then?"

I patted The Mule, glad he had asked me a question that I actually knew. "I'm not sure. But I do know that wherever I need to be, it isn't back there."

We rode on in companionable silence, making a slow trek back towards the brother's cottage.

CHAPTER 13

We reached the edge of the village when a farmer waved for us to stop. The Mule sighed, swishing his tongue around his mouth, then lowered his ears and bit Noble's horse. The horse squealed and tried to bolt, but Noble reined his horse in while I scolded The Mule. It wasn't the first time he had done this. The Mule flattened his ears at me, and I swatted him on the neck. He wanted to be home, to eat his grass and roll in the dust.

Not that I blamed him, but I wanted to hear what the farmer had to say.

"Brigid's been married."

"What?" I said, overpowering my escort's question of, "To whom?"

My head spun, and for an instant I gripped The Mule's mane tight for fear that I would fall off him. Brigid, married? It couldn't be. She would have told me that she had her eyes set on a boy. She wouldn't have been able to hide that big of a secret in a cottage so small, much less from me. The ground lurched, or seemed to, when I realized that she hadn't been able to hide it from me. In fact, I'd come all too close to finding her out. That was why she'd started to pull away from me.

Meanwhile, the farmer was oblivious to the way his news had rocked me, speaking in an animated fashion as though it were the best thing he'd heard since last service.

"The Lord's son! It seems the two of them got to know each other quite well over the winter," said the farmer with a wink.

"Melody's here," my escort said, glancing at me even as I fought to keep my stomach down in the place where it belonged. I didn't care what was said around me, anymore. What mattered was that Brigid would be living with her husband. I'd go back to a cottage with two monks in it, grow old and fat and feeble, bury them, and still be living alone in a house that echoed of times long past.

The farmer immediately cleared his throat. "All very much proper, mind you. Sanctioned visits and everything."

I didn't care if it was sanctioned visits or not, Brigid was still gone. True, I had seldom let her or anyone else know how much she mattered to me, but I thought it should have been obvious that she was the only person who could have been my companion. Now she was gone.

"Brother Adams wouldn't let a man so much as look at Brigid," I said, shaking my head. I wasn't trying to argue with the farmer. I was still trying to piece together how it had happened. How I had let it happen under my nose! The brothers had insisted upon absolute purity with me, and they'd gotten it, but I didn't know until now just how destructive absolute ignorance was.

Bile rose in my throat, unadulterated fury at the way that I had let myself be blinded, at the way that the brothers had manipulated me. At the same time, my reaction surprised me. Anger would have been normal, but not this level of it. What was at the seat of this? Was it that I felt betrayed by Brigid? Betrayed by the brothers? I wasn't sure. All I knew was that right then, my heart was thudding and my hands were shaking and I wanted to scream.

My escort cleared his throat. The farmer shifted under my glare, then said, "I came to tell you that they're cleaning out the cottage now. If you want to avoid the cleaning party, you should stay with my wife and me."

The Mule's hair under my fingers as I stroked it helped to calm my irregular breathing, then to soothe my emotional turmoil. Riding home in anger would do me no good, and possibly cause a whole lot of trouble. Particularly since I had abandoned the cottage with no notice, and they had to have been concerned for my well-being. Even Noble had thought that I was gone for good, run off to who knows where or maybe dead under a bridge. Anger on their part would be natural, and I should be in a state of mind to accept it and placate it.

My escort seemed to consider the farmer's offer, then shook his head. "It has been long enough since Melody has been home. But I will take you up on your offer."

I looked at him in surprise, realizing that he was going to observe our initial interaction and play peacemaker if need be. With the anger of the moment gone, I suddenly feared the sort of row I could cause with the brothers, and wished that he would agree to remain the entire night. "You've always stayed with us."

He half-smiled. "I don't think Brother Jacob is in any mood to entertain guests."

"But marriage is a happy occasion." I didn't finish what I was going to say. Even I knew that Brigid's marriage would cause a ruckus, but I hadn't thought that meant the brothers would be disapproving. Just because two people got married didn't mean that they'd done anything impure with each other. Both men were gazing away from me, as though they knew differently. But they hadn't lived in the house with Brigid, they hadn't lived under the yoke of Brother Adams' rules. They didn't know that it was downright impossible for Brigid to have gotten away. Why, for her to have found a man to love at all must have been in every way as challenging as for a lord to rescue a maiden from a tower.

I nudged The Mule home, not waiting for Noble to finish his conversation with the farmer. The Mule, knowing this path as the road to sweet grass and clean water, picked up his pace so fast that he would have out-trotted Noble's horse even if he had been beside us. At the bend, The Mule's sides coated in sweat and he slowed enough that Noble caught up to us. Noble gave me a nod, but his jaw was set as though he were ready to fight.

When I reached the cottage, Brigid's half-stitched cloak flew out the open door along with the words, "I never want to see trace of that girl again!"

My initial thought of running up to them and

announcing my arrival by demanding news of Brigid's marriage faded from my mind. Which girl were they speaking of? If Brigid wasn't here any longer, and the brothers truly did not want me anyway, I needed to know now. Noble could escort me for a time until I found a direction to start exploring. Still, the thought of confronting the brothers with this plan stabbed me through the chest.

As I dismounted and stripped the tack off both creatures, I heard Brother Adams say, "Come now, she's just a girl."

Belatedly, I realized that this time, it was Brother Adams who was the neutral force in the household, and Brother Jacob who was expressing his views in shouts and the tossing of random items.

"Girls! Women! Liars and betrayers, the lot of them! You feed them, you clothe them, and this is what you get in return! Faithlessness! Selfishness! Sin!" With every fourth or fifth word, something new was thrown into the dust out front: Brigid's sewing bag, a bundle of fabric, socks, a spoon she had carved, a blanket she had embroidered. Either my things had preceded this treatment, or Brother Jacob was furious with Brigid and not me. Given my initial burst of anger, I fully understood his.

"I told you we should beat them." Brother Adams' words brought my steps to a complete stop. Once or twice he had threatened to take a switch to us, but he never had. It stung to think that he would have done it, and in far greater frequency than he had threatened, if Brother Jacob had been in agreement. Should the house rules change to allow beatings, there was no way that I would set foot inside that cottage ever again.

"My father beating my mother never improved her any, but I suppose I am the fool for thinking that soft words would make a woman good!" Brother Jacob's words were bitter but much lower than his previous outbursts. If I were going to be eavesdropping any longer, I would learn so much about them that I would lose my courage to enter the house again.

I picked up a square of fabric I had been turning into a rag for my nose, and came to stand in the doorway. There wasn't a chest unopened in the entire cottage. I had so few items to start with that it was hard to tell if I still had a presence here. Piles of fabric heaped on the floor, the beds had been stripped, the book making materials were pushed into one corner of the table, sharing space with knives and bread and cheese and crumbs. Brother Jacob grabbed a pitcher and threw it upon the floor, shattering it into pieces.

"Should I stay with Mary Brown and her husband tonight?" I asked, picking up a shard of pottery which had come to rest by the door.

"Melody!" said Brother Adams.

Brother Jacob closed his eyes and muttered a word I wasn't supposed to hear, a word that frequented the less-pleasant inns that Noble had occasionally had us rest at. I walked to the table and began to sort it out, sweeping the crumbs to the floor, acting very calm and composed despite the pounding of my heart. In the silence following my arrival, I said, "I heard about Brigid getting married. Is it the three of us now?"

"Yes," Brother Jacob said. His voice sounded scratchy, as though he had been yelling at Brigid for a long time. It was exactly how I felt.

The pottage pot had the remainder of a meal in it, caked over and dry. I took it and a large wooden spoon that Jacob had carved over the winter. "Not worthy of slopping a pig," I said in disgust. "Both of you go sit down. If I see either one of you twitch a finger this evening, I'll take a switch from the willow tree and lay it on your hide."

I meant for them to know that I heard what Brother Adams had said about beating us, and I meant for them to know that I was not beyond using the same thing right back on them. When a cough came from the door, I saw Noble standing there, holding the reins to the horse he had re-saddled. A faint smile crossed his face when I nodded farewell to him. He left without further interruption.

Brother Jacob sank down onto his bed and stared at the wall. Brother Adams watched me for a time, then set to helping me clean. Just like him, though I had threatened the switch, I didn't actually follow through. There was far too much sorting out to be done to chase away a good pair of hands. After the pot was simmering and both men had bowls of sop and slices of bread, Brother Jacob looked at me and said, "You're a good woman, Melody."

"Eat. I'll be back soon," I said, taking a sack of broken housewares with me to the rubbish pit outside.

When I was far enough away from the house, I sank to the ground and began to sob. After a few minutes, I felt something hot in my hair. Reaching up, I stroked The Mule's nose and hid with him until he grew bored and wandered away.

***

Servants prepared the great hall for a feast, putting up trestle tables along the sides of the hall, then spearing candles on spikes protruding from the walls of carved panelling. The brother's cottage could have fit nicely into this hall alone four times, and likewise a fifth cottage could have been built in the white-walled courtyard scurrying with servants going to and from the kitchens, chapel, and hall. A crooked-backed man lit the chandeliers when a flurry of motion caught my gaze, and I realized Brigid was passing her white-gowned infant to me.

Brigid's movements were hampered by the tightness of her sleeves, sewn in tight to her body after she had put the pink tunic, and glimpses of the garment were seen through a side-less gray gown worn over it with gold lacing and tassels down the side. A green mantle draped over the back of her chair, too warm in the lord's house for her to wear it, but a status symbol that needed shown to her old friends nonetheless. Her face looked different with her hair covered up under a white headdress, but her expressions remained much the same as always. One of the younger women watched Brigid with envy, but all I wanted to do was cut her arms free from their binding stitches.

I cradled Brigid's baby in my arms, noticing a stain on his forehead where Brother Adams had anointed him after baptism. He smiled at me, as though he knew it had been me who got the dragon scale for his naming. The brothers had a healthy stash of scales from me collecting them when the dragons molted; unlike a living scale, the dragons did not care one way or another what someone wanted with their old cast-off scales, and the church had plenty of uses for them. This was one, to powder it and smear it during naming.

"Please, I yearn to know!" Brigid's voice was eager, and she looked healthy and strong, but most importantly, she looked happy. It made a lump form in my throat, but I couldn't deny that this life was exactly what she wanted and it fit her. "What dragon was it?"

Other women leaned forward and softened their voices, likewise wishing to know which dragon's element had been ground into a powder, mixed with neatsfoot oil, and placed upon his skin to absorb. The two brothers could not tell one dragon scale from the next, but I could. I knew each of the dragons scales by sight, by smell, and by texture, and I knew the positive and negative attributes that the dragons could pass onto the children. It was not often that I spoke the name or the type of dragon, but sometimes I did. I whispered to Brigid, "Ragnark."

Brigid gasped and glowed all the more. The months that had passed between her marriage and now had given me time to accept her change in position, but life with the brothers wasn't the same. With her gone, the rules were gone, as well as many of the restrictions, but I saw in their eyes this wasn't because they trusted me, but because Brigid had broken them. They felt they had failed her, even as she took up the role of one of the most important women in the kingdom. It also meant that they had cut out all meaningful communication with me, and were petrified should I mention leaving.

"It is who I want my child anointed after." I smiled at the thought. We were all in the hall, sitting on two benches facing a central fire back against the wall, and from my position next to the baby and mother, I was in a prime location for everyone to stare at me. This thought had not occurred to me when Brigid had insisted that I sit next to her after the naming ceremony was complete.

"He is perfect, isn't he?" said a woman with fingers currently bright blue from dying wool in woad. The old servant man sniffed and looked away at the sight of the dyer's fingers, and I had a feeling that the servants had been informed to treat the working women with dignity, even though some of them were having trouble complying with the orders. Praise for the child filled the naked silence, then followed calculated conversation, my mistake reminding everyone to mind what they said.

Don't taint her. Careful; she's more sensitive than a child. I saw the warning pass between each woman as someone brought up the subject of cooking. It was neutral until someone mentioned using butter, a luxury I was not allowed, and then the conversation died again.

A twitch of pain entered my friend's eyes, and the entreating of the ladies after Brigid's secret came to a sudden close. They shifted uncomfortably. I realized the nagging doubts in my mind were right. I wasn't going to have a child. Not now, not ever. The drunk had been telling me the truth when I had encountered him in a rare moment when I was unguarded by an escort: Virgins can't have babies.

The old man's foot caught on the rail of a step ladder and he tilted. A young man who had been watching him immediately sprang to catch him, but the ladder was overturned and fell to the ground with a clatter. Instantly, the women who had come to see Brigid in her finery were on their feet, tending to the man, sorting out his ladder and asking fifteen times how he felt. It gave me some breathing space. I needed to speak to Brigid, to ask her a question that had been burning me for such a long time.

I eased closer to Brigid, and she showed me how to swaddle her child, how to hold it. Settled at last, I began to say, "During the last hunt, something strange happened..."

But Brigid shook her head. "You can't speak to me of such things any longer. You shouldn't speak to me at all."

I wanted to stand up or snap at her, but the child in my arms had let out a long yawn and shifted in his blanket. I watched him until he stuck his tongue out of his lips and his eyes drifted shut again. Odd how every naming ceremony I attended stung my heart harder than the last. Odd how I wished that the last dragon had refused to relinquish me, after all.

My friend did not immediately take her son back into her arms. "You can hold him longer. He's sleeping well."

It was a reminder that this was as close as I would come to having a babe. My face blushed hot. "I'm jealous, Brigid. I'm not allowed to marry."

"Melody, that's not true."

I glanced at the other women, who were by now seating the man on a chair and checking his head while two other ladies set about finishing the lighting of the chandelier. Admittedly, they seemed more interested in getting close to that much silver than they did in helping the man in his duties. Something that had been eating at me became painfully obvious: As long as I was virgin, I was the sacrifice, and I kept their daughters safe. They would say and do anything to keep me in my place. They'd done it all my life. They would tell me any number of things. First it was that I was too young, then that I had to understand myself, then that all the eligible men were affianced, and suddenly their words turned irritated. They now said I was too old for a husband, too old to endure the child bed. They would tell me that my life is esteemed and the highest station a woman could dare dream for. They would say I brought great glory and honor, that I saved lives I otherwise would not be able to.

I said, "Brigid."

Her bright eyes found mine, piercing my will the way her hand had once stilled unicorns. She only said, "I have sullied you. It is due to me that you missed the unicorn."

I tried to soothe Brigid with a pat on the hand. Whatever had happened to make the monster come for me, it was not due to Brigid. I told her, "It happens, from time to time."

She pulled away from me and glared. "Not to you. And not to Brother Jacob. I did not wish to speak with you about this, but I must." Brigid caught the gaze of a gray-haired woman before looking at her child in my arms and saying, "That is your son. Every child you have saved over the years is yours, as truly as they are the flesh of their parents."

I should have known better than to express interest in having my own babe as well. Though the dragons had taught me to sit and listen even when I did not want to, I knew this was one thing I could not bear to hear again. "If you believe such a thing, you will look in my eyes and tell me with all conviction that the love you feel for your son is the same as the love you feel for every other child you have rescued."

Brigid met my challenge, but her eyes held none of the piercing quality, and she couldn't voice the words she mouthed.

"Melody," it was Brother Adams' voice. "It is time for us to retire."

I went along quietly, allowing him to hold out my cloak for me. He had come along at a good time; I didn't know what else I had to say to Brigid. I brushed my cheek against the unicorn fur lining the cloak, taking comfort from the way that Noble had come through for me. He said the abbot had even blessed it before sending it to me.

"Melody," Brigid said, standing suddenly right behind me.

I smoothed my face in the smile that Brother Jacobs used when he was faking serenity. "Brigid, congratulations again. I hope to come see you soon."

From the old servant's scowl at my words, I knew that my wishes would be likely to remain a hope and nothing more. The older they were, the better they knew what their masters approved of, and this class of women friends were not suitable for an aristocratic woman. Then Brother Jacob towered over me, and the two shepherded me out of the lord's hall and into the chill of autumn. As we crossed the drawbridge and stepped around the village I had never spent much time in, I wondered how much of the conversation the brothers had heard.

A wind curled my cloak about my calves, and Brother Adams said, "The child is full term."

"Mmm." Brother Jacob was never one to talk much. I usually had my meaningless conversations with Brother Adams, but I wasn't feeling up to the task now, not when everything that came out of his lips grated against my skin. I tasted the air instead. Winter would come early.

"She was wed after Easter," Brother Adams continued, emphasizing the words as though they should mean something.

The woods were unusually quiet, and no birds sang nor did squirrels clamber onto the gnarled fingers of limbs to chatter at us. Nothing had been right since this last unicorn, and I had yet to settle my mind upon what would set it right. I'd tried several things, but found none of them satisfactory.

"When we had to go to another valley for a feast," Brother Adams jabbed these words at me. Or perhaps it was at Brother Jacob, but Adams still sought to pin some blame on me as well. Ever since Brigid had been wed, Brother Adams hadn't been the same. He'd turned vindictive. "That was five months ago."

Five months? It meant I had six more before we went on the next Easter hunt. Time did not matter to me the way it mattered to farmers for planting, nor to tax men for gathering the annual tithes. To me, time was from one Easter hunt to the next, a time when I struggled to survive the elements as well as the horn and hooves of our quarry.

"Humiliations!" Brother Adams puffed out his chest like a dragon preparing to flame. "The child's been born a month already! What a scandal, the whole of the village is—"

I interrupted him, irritated that once again this was rubbing on my ignorance. "What scandal could there be? Brigid is fortunate to have born the babe at her age, much less to have been gifted with him so early into her marriage. Women two Easters married have yet to be so blessed."

Brother Jacob sent Adams a glare over the top of my head, and another round of silence spun around me. The crunch of leaves filled the air. As though to remedy the situation, Brother Jacob said to me, "You are very fortunate, Anna, to not have to fret for your life every year in the child bed."

A barking laugh came from my slightly hoarse throat. Once again they called me Anna! Did I remind them so much of her that they couldn't resist the urge, or did they worry I would follow her path? Anger made my voice sharp. "Indeed, I merely have to wonder every year if the unicorn will find me worthy to lay his head in my lap or stab me through the heart, and every few years I go with dragons. Certainly my role is so much safer."

Brother Adams made a strangled noise as though I had punched him in the gut. A sigh hissed out of Brother

Jacob. Lifting up my chin, I searched the skies for a glimpse of stars through branches with the remnants of leaves still clinging to them. The dragons had told me of constellations, and I found the guiding star named Dunoon. Ages and ages the dragon had lived, and so much he had seen. I had a fraction of his life, and I wished to see some of what he had.

I said, "I want to go out into the world."

Brother Adams knew to watch me closely after I returned from dragons; they liked to talk, and lately their lectures had been changing me as I pondered their lessons for longer periods at a time. Brother Jacob spoke with an air of indifference. "If you wish a walk by yourself, you may take the long route. Brother Adams will have supper ready when you arrive."

My fingers found a hole in my dress, one I had missed while mending the day before. "I do not mean I wish to go for a walk. I want something besides *this*. To be an embroiderer or a weaver."

Anything but a virgin.

The entire way home, I had been thinking of the occupations most likely to be accepted as a replacement for sacrifice, and those were the two I thought would be seen as the most likely. I would be happy to settle into life as a trades person, rearing fat babies like the one Brigid had. It was one of the few things I hadn't yet tried. Tending to children seemed like a good use for me, and I wanted them to be my own.

A stern voice cut through my thoughts as Brother Jacob tested me. "You are the virgin. If you desire to embroider, I will see a teacher brought to our services."

Though I was accustomed to having my will tempered to something far more humble than my intent, I felt a ripple of anger at these words. I had accepted that butter, spices, and salt was a luxury not to be partaken of, but this—to be told I couldn't leave? I had not responded to him. Not until I pried my elbow out of his grasp, my blood simmering. "Is it not well past time that my station be surrendered to another? Surely I am the oldest virgin in all the mountains?"

Even in the moonlight, I could see I had angered him. Brother Adams folded his hands before his body and seemed to be speaking to the passing rose bushes. "Virginity is an occupation, a state of mind, spirit, and body. It knows no age. It is healthy to question your faith, but for now you must think—think hard, and upend that seed of evil the dragon has placed within your soul. Do you not keep the villages safe?"

I closed my eyes, knowing I was dangerously close to losing my freedom for the next month. Just seeing Brigid had put them both into an odd mood, and I would bet that it would take very little to make them reinstate the rules I had so hated. I admitted, "I do."

They must have been tired, for neither one of them decided to question the tone of my voice. Brother Adams continued, "Do you not serve as a righteous, pure image to which all females should aspire?"

I gritted my teeth. "I should think that the women to be aspired towards exist in the Good Word."

We paused in front of the cottage door. Had both men not been shivering in their worn tunics, I might have been reprimanded on this point, but instead they entered the cottage. Brother Jacob knelt before banked coals and started a fire with twigs. They allowed a fire at night, and when they needed the heat to cure their books. Conveniently, they tried to do their book making during the winter times when the books required both the light and the heat. It was a good excuse to stay warm, but it meant we were not as pious as other people.

Brother Adams said, "I mean, aren't you a physical embodiment of what a woman should be?"

Casting my eyes to the fire which burned much colder than the one the dragons made for me at night, I said, "I suppose."

Brother Jacob spoke as he tossed a small log onto the tender flames. "Is your work not good?"

"It is good." I lied by imbuing conviction in my voice which I did not feel. After seeing Brigid, even I felt changed. Tired, worn, and irritated. Like there was an itch I wasn't allowed to ease, or a pain in my foot that they denied existed.

"Are you not provided for? Do you not have respect, honor, and dignity reserved only for the most esteemed of your sex? How many women envy your freedom! You have such access to books and you worry not for marital disputes and after ill children. Your status is most high. Would you abandon your exalted rank for a harlot's role?"

Anger rippled through me, and then indignation, for as he professed respecting and honoring me, I found his manner so condescending that I would have sooner mistaken him for the dragon and the dragon for him. I did not dare to say this, and nor did I dare to let my emotions or thoughts show upon my face.

I bowed my head, seemingly to find my footing in the dark. Brother Adams took me to prayer, where I laid prone upon the floor and found no peace. Eve had plucked fruit from the tree of knowledge. If she had not, would we have these books, these stories, this religion? Or would we be in the Garden of Eden, complacent as the sheep dragons ate for dinner?

The next day, I stood on a bridge after a rain, and I watched the water run beneath the bridge, taking leaves and logs alike in its tumbling greed. I stared at the water, at the way it swallowed up all in its path, wore it down, broke it to its will, using whatever it wished as it wished to.

The water was like these villages, encompassing me, turning me to their will, using me and paying no heed to where I may want to go or what I may want to do. So long as I was in the water, I would not get out alive. It would seem, I had to find a way out of the water. But how? Where was I to go, and what was I to do?

It was then that my heart spoke to me again, and this time I listened to it.

CHAPTER 14

My stomach stirred as I slipped on my cloak, unicorn fur pressing against my shoulders, catching the musky scent of dragon scales used in the embroidery.

"I am going out," I told the monks hunched over their books. I feared they would hear the quiver in my voice. I grasped the tooth on my necklace. "I may be a week or two."

Brother Adams looked up from pulling string through the binding of his book, and Brother Jacob from laying out a letter upon the page, calculating the placement of a 'G' before touching the hide with anything permanent. He had already scraped off the mistakes once today. Brother Adams said, "Melody, this is not to do with what that woman said to you?"

My heart stilled. That's what they called Brigid now. 'That woman'. It had everything to do with what she had said. I might have allowed her to persuade me, but when I had looked into my friend's eyes I had seen guilt, and when I had looked into my own heart, I had seen green eyes and a barren road.

I picked up my basket and said, "No."

"Melody," said Brother Adams again, his voice patient but strained. "Come speak with me."

I glanced at them. Brother Jacob was irritated, as I had expected, and Brother Adams was leaning towards me.

I could see what was going to happen: Brother Adams would draw me under his arm and listen to me next to the fire. When my temper or tears or composed statement had run its course, he would tell me all was forgiven and lapse into prayer, and Brother Jacob would administer one of his sermons until *I* was asking *them* for forgiveness, which they would heavily and solemnly grant, reminding me of the gifts I had been blessed with in this life of comfort: Books, a warm fire, a roof, no husband to beat me, no threat of dying on the child bed.

Brother Adams gave his fellow a sigh and began to put down his work. I lifted my chin and embraced the trembles coursing through my body. Winter would lock me in, unless I acted now. If Brother Adams put his hand on my shoulder, I would freeze at his touch, the way a unicorn did at mine.

"If we are to have another winter like last, this will be the final chance to gather what herbs remain," I said.

I knew that after days, weeks, or months passed, a rider would come, his horse run so hard it would fall over dead, sometimes miles out of town, and the villagers would carry his message to us. Brother Jacob would command order and hear of the nature of the evil. He would send word to Lord Richmond, who would dispatch an escort and a horse for me. I would secretly stash a knife and red dragon scale amid a basket with cheese and bread, and I would pull my cloak on my shoulders. When I rode out of the village, the people would gather and watch, glad that it was I who was leaving and not one of their own.

Brother Jacob heaved a sigh. He knew the stocks of herbs and the ways of a healing touch. Brother Adams looked to him, silently asking if they needed the herbs. I locked eyes with Brother Jacob.

An eternity stretched before us. It was Brother Jacob who was with me on the Easter hunts, when the fasting sometimes lasted weeks while I waited and purified my thoughts. Brother Jacob who would be as a wolf in the woods, following at a distance, watching my every move, listening to my every song and hymn. It was he who witnessed the cold of the night and the pain in my bare feet. It was he who held his breath when the beast came and laid its head in my lap. It was he who drew back the arrow and pierced the unicorn through its heart. It was he who had fallen asleep last spring, and it was I who had taken the blame for it. And now, it was he who looked away. He resumed scratching on his book, his tone broken when he said, "Let her go."

"What?" Brother Adams said. He had been certain of a different answer. They knew that something had changed over the years; the unicorn, my runaway, then my friend's conversation, each one chipping away at a world the Brothers could never set right again. Brother Adams took a step towards me.

"I said, let her go!" Brother Jacob nearly shouted the words. Swallowing, Brother Jacob looked at his shaking hand. He had gouged deep grooves into the page. He said, softly, "We can always use more herbs.|

Breathing suddenly coming rapid, I could not look at the man slumped over his book with his head in his hands. I lowered my head, and slipped through the door, knowing he knew I was leaving to lose my virginity.

Blood pounded through my veins as I leaned against the shut door, breathing in wood smoke coming from the cottage. Panic was setting in. Where would I go? I knew no one who would shelter me without locking the doors upon me and turning me in. A good virgin was hard to find, was the prize of all prizes, and though Brother Jacob had slipped last Easter, the unicorn had still come to me.

I shivered beneath my cloak, not cold, just frightened. I could endure snow and frost easily with the hide of a unicorn wrapped around me, but what about a longer duration? I did have money, baubles and silver and gold bits won from games with dragons, but that would only last for so long. It might be enough for a cottage somewhere, but an unwed woman with so much wealth and no family would draw attention.

That was assuming I found a man to claim my maidenhead. How was a woman to lose it? What did she ask for? Did she ask, or was the man to come to her? Why did she need a man, besides? No one had spoken to me of such things. I'd overheard many a hushed joke, enough to rise my suspicions.

Once, I had asked Brother Jacob if the thing I was to avoid was the sort of behavior the rams and ewes did over the summer up in the mountains. He had given me a confused "What?" and I had given him a detailed account of a ram mounting a ewe. To this, Brother Jacob had said that there were differences between men and beasts, and would say nothing more on the subject.

Before anyone could come out of the cottage looking for me, I pushed off the door and set my feet on a game trail, feeling with every step an increasing sense of loss, worry that I would be returned, and the breath-stealing terror of not knowing what to do next.

My fear of the dark had never truly receded, and I found myself constantly checking around the meandering trails to be certain the noises were from deer or foxes. A chill crept up my back, and I couldn't shake the feeling that even now something was following me at a distance. I held my head up and hurried, reminding myself constantly that as ignorant as I was in the ways of men, I was every bit as wise in the ways of wild and magic. A little bit of darkness had nothing on me.

Yet still I shivered, and thought I saw the bushes up on the ridge move without wind.

I cut across the pasture, and once again, The Mule lifted his head, grunted, and followed me.

More than once I wondered what I was doing, but I didn't stop or turn back. Instead, I thought I would avoid the places where men might hear of my flight and be watching for me. When I was far enough away, I would nestle down in some small community who had never heard of the woman who had tamed dragons and yet didn't know how babies came into being. Someone would teach me, but I needed to never admit to my past for fear of being returned to it.

The mountains passed slowly around me as the day wore on. No travellers were upon the roads, but I avoided them anyway.

I found a berry patch just off the trail, big clusters of blackberries in a swampy dip in the ground. My hands and arms bore the brunt of thorns, but I continued to pick and eat until I was contented. It took a long time, but I did not mind until I heard the squirrels stop the chattering and go silent.

I stopped picking berries and eyed the tree line. Was there someone following me?

Then I saw him, a white beast with a horn as long as my arm. He was the height of a plough horse and every bit as large, muscles quivering as he smelled the air. We stared at one another. He tossed his head and stepped back into shadows, melding with the fabric of the forest.

I shivered and pressed down the trail faster, noticing when the ground became hard and frozen beneath my feet. There was the scent of snow on the wind, still distant. Or so I hoped. I took to the roads, feeling a little more at ease when I had not spied the unicorn in some time.

Only once the mud sucked at my boots on an ill-used path did I feel the cautious conversation fade from my ears and the half-pitying, half-accusing glares release their hold on my back.

Many days and nights I guarded myself under my cloak before I woke one morning and it was warmer. The storm would come that day, and it would be a bad one. I needed to find shelter, no matter who might see me.

Sullied. That was the word Brigid had used. They thought that despite their best efforts to keep me pure, I had been sullied. Was it Brigid who had so-sullied me, or was it something I overheard?

I must have been sullied. That must be what happened. Why else would the monster pursue me?

I pushed into the only inn in the village, a trail of snow blowing through the door and sending a chill through huddles of red-cheeked customers. Five people glared at me before I ducked my head and snaked towards the inn keeper. I was shaking when I saw a bear of a man snarling at another man entirely too drunk for the hour. Breathing in and out, I told myself I could do this, just a few lines. I'd seen Noble making these transactions before, and I had coin from Ragnark's hoard.

I stood up straighter and met the innkeeper's eye, trying to be firm and failing. "Do you have a room for the night?"

The man passed a cursory glance over my apparel, noting the embroidery but not the scales, thinking the fur lining my cloak to be hare. He chewed an oat stem, switching it from one side to the next as he thought. "'ow many in your party?"

"Me." I grasped Ragnark's tooth on my necklace out of habit. It had cut through a dragon's foot once, when I had been pinned down in a lair. Soft flesh such as a man's would give way easily. "I will have a safe place to sleep and something hot to eat and drink. I don't mind what."

No matter what the innkeeper served, it would be an improvement over the brother's fare. I sorely missed my mother's cooking, and wished that I would have paid more attention when she made her meals. Learning to cook from the brothers had not been a boon to my skills.

The man spat into a rag, then tucked that into his belt. "Don't 'ave a single room."

"Do you have anything at all?" While I was willing to weather a small snow storm, what was brewing outside would be up to my knees tomorrow and possibly up to my waist the day after. Shelter was my best option.

"It's shared or you can sleep on the hearth. Or try to." The man studied me from eyes to waist, seeming to judge me as someone who would not fare well with that crowd, then said, "I know company who will keep hands to themselves."

My gaze shifted to the blazing fire where patrons crowded one another, cheering and thumping drinks, many of them already having had more ale than they could handle. Women in low cut-dresses flirted with the merchant men, and I saw at least one guest with light fingers. Virgin I may be, but I was no fool. Without another second, I reached into my purse and withdrew a couple of coins, a smaller amount than my escort would have paid.

The innkeeper huffed. "That your offer? Even with me going out of the way?"

"Yes, it is. And I have a mule outside. He needs cared-for." My gaze darted to his, and I looked into his eyes.

The price had not displeased him; he had been trying to squeeze more money from my fingers. He swished the oat stem to the other side of his mouth and said, "Come with me."

I followed him to a table in the corner. It was farthest from the fire, but the heat from the kitchen penetrated the wall. I glanced around while the innkeeper spoke to the two men and saw that with the activity of the inn, I would have had to come to this table to find a place to sit.

He started an easy banter, cutting it short when his portly missus brushed past him with four pints of frothy ale and a glare. The innkeeper stated his purpose. Once the men had agreed to share their room three ways, the innkeeper scurried off. I sat in a chair with my back to the fire.

The men had an air of friendship about them, despite nearly a generation age difference. Gray hair could be seen amidst the golden hair of the taller man, and he drank a beer as dark as his eyes.

The other man nearly blended into the wood, his skin the darkened hue of a traveller and his wavy brown hair matted slightly from time spent in the wind. His green eyes had the laughter of magic in them, and I saw in the way he tore off a chunk of bread the easy movements of a sorcerer.

"Did you order yourself anything to eat, miss?" the blond asked. I recognized his gentle tones immediately as the same ones that my escorts had; whoever he was, this man was from the castle. "You look as though you have not eaten well in days."

"I did, and I assure you I have eaten as well as one might," I said, forgetting to use a rougher tongue the way I did when I was with Noble in these types of places. True, inns catered to those who could afford it, but the were seldom as educated as I was.

"What is your name, come my child, I shall not withhold my friendship with such a charming creature."

Creature is more accurate than you dare to dream, I thought, but only gave him a smile. A bowl of hot beef broth appeared over my shoulder, and a cup of spiced cider. The innkeeper was trying to impress someone, and I was not sure if that someone was me or the men. I thanked the innkeeper, and accepted the slice of bread the nobleman cut.

"My name is Melody." The only way my name could be more common was if it was 'Mary', so I did not fear discovery if the brothers had changed their minds and decided to send out riders for me.

"Honored. My friend goes by the name Warin, and I am Lord Richmond."

A hot rush flowed through my veins and I tried to not panic. That made him my liege, the ruler of the land, the man whose services I had ultimately been escaping, barring the king himself. It was every bit my sort of luck that I should run right to the very thing I was trying to avoid, so I should not have found it such a surprise. "Might I ask what has you in these parts so late in the fall, milord?"

Richmond's gaze drifted to the man next to him, and said, "Only the heavy business of the land."

I ate bread soaked in the beef broth, savoring the flavor and glad for chunks of meat and carrot. The men allowed me to eat and drink in silence, and we listened to those around us, enraptured in tales. When a man told of seeing the prints of a massive unicorn, he was cajoled into silence, the other men declaring the prints belonged to those of an ox.

But I knew well the difference between unicorn and

ox, and from the lines appearing around Warin's brow, he did, too. He asked, "Have you seen it?"

To suddenly have the mage speak startled me. I knew that voice, and couldn't believe I had missed recognizing his eyes. When I looked back at him, I saw the faint glimmer of a spell about the both of them. It smelled sweet, like myrrh, and I suspected that spell had been to render them both less recognizable. Add to this the years that had passed since I'd seen the mage and the short nature of our encounter, it was no wonder it had taken me so long to place him.

"Have you seen it?" the mage—Warin, that was his name, though it felt like cheating to have Lord Richmond tell me it—repeated again, slowly as though I were daft.

"Seen what?"

"The unicorn."

Ah, yes, we were talking about the unicorn before I had been distracted, thinking about the first time I'd met him. But why didn't I feel that connection again, the one I'd felt with him earlier? Was it gone, or had it always been a bit of fancy made up on my part? Now Richmond's eyes were upon me, too, studying me with intent. Get my wits about me, I was being watched, I mentally reprimanded myself while I took a long sip of cider. I shrugged and admitted, "I did see something a time or two, and it was no deer."

"We hunt the beast," Warin said. His eyes locked on mine, and the magic in them like lightning across a night sky caught my breath in my lungs. He was beautiful. Seldom had I thought a man such, but it was how I found him. There was the connection. I felt it again, this time it struck me in the belly and warmed my blood even as it chilled my fingers.

"Warin," warned Lord Richmond, misinterpreting my reaction. "Do not frighten her."

Warin's eyes studied mine, and his brow narrowed. Did he recognize me, now, too? Could he? It had been so long since we'd met. "But she must be frightened. She is the only one we have yet found with the right allure."

"You do not mean to say you plan to take her with us?" Lord Richmond frowned at Warin, then eased back into his chair, resigned. "She's too old."

"Allure knows no age. She is the right one." His words made my breath hitch. Was that admission to knowing me, to calling me the right one for him? My dress seemed to tighten on its own, as though servants had crept up behind me and stitched the bodice to my skin the way they had closed up Brigid's sleeves. Then Warin looked away, as though bored of me and of the conversation. "It is your duty to persuade her."

Bored of me, was he? Indignant pride rose to my cheeks, but also a sly grin as I decided I would discover how to play his game. I felt as though I was once more upon a dragon's doorstep, bargaining with the beast, challenging it to alter whatever plans it had had for me. It had been so long since I'd had a good opponent. Calmly, I spoke to Warin. "No gold or silver or gems of the earth could persuade me to go with you. Tell me what have you that I could possibly desire?"

Though it was an odd thing, to have gone so long yearning to meet him again, I knew that my words were true. I didn't want riches. If I were going with him, I wanted something much more valuable, and I wanted to know if he was available to give it. At this, there was a trickle of amusement upon his face and he looked at me again. "If you shall not go, you may be convinced to come with us with a reminder to your allegiance to your lord."

I cocked my head; this was not an angle any of the dragons had ever held over me before. It was also entirely aside from the matter between me and him. "This is true, and therefore I *must* go no matter my circumstances."

"What are your circumstances, miss?" Lord Richmond asked.

"Nothing of significance, milord. I shall accompany you."

Warin's brows narrowed when I directed the "you" specifically at Lord Richmond, excluding Warin from my statement. I mentally berated myself for baiting Warin, since him actually recognizing me might well lead to him taking me back to the brothers himself, or at least revealing my true identity as best as he knew it to Lord Richmond. Those green eyes lingered on me and he opened his mouth to say something when the innkeeper interrupted us by bringing a second round of broth and drink and another loaf of bread, the entire while apologizing profoundly for not having a more suitable meal. I ate all I had room in my stomach for, and asked Lord Richmond if he knew the continuation to a ballad I had once heard only part of. This sufficiently put a stop to any questions the men had about me.

Though I was exhausted, sleep did not come to me that

night as I laid awake, listening to Richmond's snores on the mattress beside me. The room was a double, and two cots were all which there was space for. Warin sat with his back against the door. I couldn't tell if he was sleeping. One thing I did know was my thoughts were keeping me awake. Thoughts of Warin. Thoughts of his lips on my wrist. And then the heady memory of the dream.

What was it like to kiss properly? I pressed my lips to my palm, then licked it, ran my tongue over the roof of my mouth and my teeth. Not sensing any extraordinary responses, I shrugged mentally. Maybe it was merely a ritual. I wondered what power my curves held to make men stare so?

What did lovers do behind closed doors? What happened between a kiss and a bulging belly? No one had so far been so casual as to make mention of this, even though they did not know that such topics were not fit for my ears. I feared more than ever the unguarded stare of men. I did not know the expression of what I'd heard the Brothers call lust, but I knew well the hungry eyes of a wolf eyeing its prey, and I saw more and more men give me that expression as of late. It's as though they can smell me, as sure as a unicorn can. I shuddered.

"You need your rest," came Warin's voice at my elbow, bringing me back to reality with a jolt, bringing a blush to my cheeks. To think that Warin was so close, yet I didn't dare to let him know me.

"Won't we wake our friend?" I asked, but was glad to have someone to speak with. I had missed the dragons, but I missed Brigid more. And I hated this gut-twisting sensation that made me think my good luck had been foiled by Lord Richmond's presence.

"He sleeps soundly, therefore I cannot." Warin paused, then drew on the floorboards. A faint trail of magic followed his fingers as he completed a symbol, a protection rune I had once seen in a book before the tutor took it away from me. "Melody."

Though I'd never been fond of my name, I loved the way it sounded on his tongue, the way he said it as though it were poetry and a spell wrapped into one word. Once again, my dress felt too tight to let me breathe properly. "Yes?"

"What are you doing so far from your protectors?"

"You do recognize me, then." It was a relief while also a concern, excitement matched up with dread. My breath locked in my throat as I waited for him to say something, anything, while I dreaded what those words might be.

Lord Richmond snored and turned onto his side, the cot creaking beneath his bulk. In the distance, past the door which lead to the hallway which lead to the inn, cheering and thumping of drinks sounded still by those who were nursing yet another drink and clinging onto whatever shreds of wakefulness that was about them.

The rustle of fabric as Warin changed position to look at me better, then my heart stopped at the intensity of his eyes, at the thick huskiness in his voice. "I could never forget you. Not in two lifetimes, not in a hundred. Your eyes have haunted me since we met."

Thrill pounded through my body, made my head float and my body quiver. If there was a way to let him know how much I agreed with him, how much I felt the same, then I wanted to let him know it. However, my mind wasn't working well enough to say all of that. I could only force a whisper. "I wish you'd taken me with you."

Those green eyes closed, and for several painful seconds, I dreaded that I was in my bed in the brother's cottage and that I was only dreaming a dream of his eyes, and when I woke up, all of this would be gone again.

Then Warin's voice came, raspy. "If I had, then you wouldn't be here with us now. What happened in the time I've been gone? The monks would have nudged you out of their care not long after I saw you. Who did you go with? What did you do?"

He would have been correct in his statements, had I been an ordinary girl. To tell him the truth would be to tell him too much. I murmured, "I don't wish to speak of it."

Warin was quiet, as though debating if he should press me for a better answer or just let me be and accept my reluctance for what it was. At last, he said, "We need you, Melody."

I wanted to hear him say that he needed me. Not that they needed me, that Lord Richmond needed my skills, my body, and my virginity the same way that he'd always used them. Even though Warin hadn't said those words to injure me, I felt the sting anyway, and my voice reflected my mood. "You won't touch me, then."

A rough inhalation, as though I had hurt him, then came Warin's soft admission. "No. I shouldn't have touched you back then. You deserve a better man than me."

Bitterly, I said, "Maybe if you knew what all I've done,

you wouldn't say that."

Warin was concerned now, and I heard the rustle of fabric as he sat up straighter. "Why? What have you done?"

"Nothing that you need to know about," I snapped, stopping myself from adding *since you're not good enough for me* when Lord Richmond snorted. I froze, hoping that I had not woken the man. My cheeks blazed.

Warin waited for the man's breathing to become regular again, and when he next spoke his voice had lost the musical quality. "You'll tell me in time, since we will remain here until the storm has lessened."

My voice still kept its edge, but with it was a hint of mirthful laughter to think that I knew something of magic that the mage did not. "Then I shall leave without you. I have no desire to winter in this village."

"How do you know the storm will not let up?"

I knew because I *knew*, but that answer would raise too many questions. So far he knew only my name, that I was pure, and that I had at one time been watched over by Brother Jacob. If he wanted nothing else from me than to use me the same way the rest of the kingdom did, then perhaps he really wasn't good enough for me. This meant the more he knew of me, the harder I would find it to slip away again. How long did it take a bruised heart to heal, I wondered. To pacify him, I said, "I know the mountains. We must finish the climb over the pass, or none of us shall remove from here."

A long stretch of silence followed my statement, filled with open-mouthed snores. Warin looked at me, and I saw that his eyes cast a faint glow in the dark. "I understand you desire to keep your own counsel, and so you may. But you have the look of magic about you, and I want to know if there is anything you need to tell me about your past."

Like I was going to tell him anything about my past now that he'd rejected me? I set my lips in a thin line, not caring that he couldn't see, and said, "The beast follows me. That is all."

"Then that is well in my mind." From the way that he said it, though, it was not well in his mind at all, rather the opposite. I set my jaw and refused to let my lips move to even form other words. Warin paused, then said, "You ask too few questions for my comfort."

"You said I could keep my own counsel." I managed to not spit his own words back at him, but it was a conscious effort. I would not let him know he had made me angry. It was like letting a dragon know. It was a way to lose a bit of ground in our stalemate.

The door rattled as he let his head fall back against it. "I was not expecting you to do so." His tone was annoyed, as though I had been the one who pushed him away.

My nostrils flared when my instinct was to reconcile with him. Why wouldn't my own mind allow me to have the final word? Why did I feel like I had to respond to him? I swallowed these thoughts. "What is it you would like to know?"

"Why do you keep a gryphon claw around your neck?"

Disappointment welled in my chest. Of all the things to ask, he had to ask about what I wore around my neck? What was about my neck? I reached up and felt it, realizing what was talking about. Ragnark's tooth. It was not a gryphon claw, but he had not asked me what it was, merely why. If I were less mad at him, I would have set him straight. I instead answered his misinformed question without correcting him. "It was given to me."

Warin was quiet in response. I forbade myself to look over at him again, instead turning my back to him. How could we be two people who knew, with absolute certainty, that we knew each other long ago, yet now we knew each other less than two strangers? Lord Richmond's snores were louder now. It took a long, long time before I could find any sleep.

CHAPTER 15

We made as fine of a company as any I had seen, two riding horses and The Mule with supplies purchased prior to leaving the village for good. Lord Richmond sat upon a bay with a stripe down his face and a single white stocking on a foreleg, while Warin rode the same black horse as had escaped him and caused me to meet him years ago.

This time, the black horse stood relaxed but alert, his hide marked with bald scars upon his chest and hind quarters, as though he had seen fights. Compared to the slick-coated, muscled steeds, my mule looked down-trodden and exhausted even though I knew his strength would continue for longer than my own did.

Despite Lord Richmond's inquiries, there was not even a spare plough horse to be purchased and so we had to be contented with two mounts and three people. The Mule served his use by shouldering the packs of the two horses, presumably as a way to guilt me into remaining with them. Upon seeing us move out, a few other travellers took to the rode as well, muttering curses at the snow about their knees.

A quick meal of porridge, heavy on the water and light on the oats, had proven to be an awkward, silent affair as Warin and I had a non-verbal stand off. Even though he never said so, I knew he was angry with me for having rejected him earlier, and I was angry at him for being angry, and angry at myself, and upset with him for pretending that he wasn't so much as tempted to kiss my hand. Part of me wondered if he was showing me what rejection was like, and that made me all the more resentful. So I walked behind Lord Richmond's bay, but in front of Warin's black.

For a time, we passed over flat fields coated in a blanket of snow, the road itself half-melted and in places, the bare pebbles of the road showed through the white fluff. Back at the inn, I had oiled my shoes and leg wrappings in preparation for this long walk.

Lord Richmond had offered me the bay to ride, but The Mule had chosen that instant to chomp the horse's neck and frighten the poor bay into a quivering sheen of sweat. Warin suggested The Mule was jealous and that I should walk him until he had tired. Or that I ride behind him on his black horse, and tie The Mule to his saddle. Riding behind Warin would bring me into contact with the mage, and I was still too annoyed with him to give him that pleasure. So I walked, leading The Mule without the need for halter or rope, much to Richmond's admiration.

In time, we passed over a solid bridge crossing a creek which was ice of dubious thickness, and I was reminded of childhood stories of trolls living beneath such bridges. However, in my life and travels, I had yet to encounter a troll, unless rough vagabonds huddled over smoky fires could be considered trolls. The Mule cropped at the occasional stand of tall grass with a pile of snow at its base, and soon the familiarity of our pace and the chatter of birds between storms soothed me into a peaceful wandering. My skirts, even tied up at the knee, began to dampen, and I was glad for the oil on my shoes and leg wrappings to keep the bite of snow at bay.

Then the landscape shifted as we left behind the easy fields and came to the start of a mountain pass. While Richmond halted his horse, studying the mountain for sign of the trail winding through trees, I passed him up and kept on the path, knowing these roads as well as a dragon knows hunting grounds in his dragonhaunt.

"Will you ride behind me?" Richmond asked once we had travelled perhaps two miles. I was leading the pack mule on foot, picking out a trail in the slippery landscape. Richmond's horse was coated in sweat, and I knew it would hold up better without the extra weight.

"No," I said, "though I thank you for your kindness, I fear it would be a disservice to your steed. The ground is uneven and it is work enough without me."

"Certainly you are cold and wet?"

I was, despite my precautions, very wet now. It might have been due to sweating from exertion, or the snow had worn away the oil of my boots. Pausing, I leaned against The Mule and considered. We were making slow progress, but I could not see myself moving any faster without the creatures in tow, and I would only grow cold by sitting inactive on a horse. The birds had stopped their singing, and I couldn't see any other travellers when I looked back towards the village we had just left. Night would fall in a few hours, and travel would be less than ideal. I pointed to the low dip in the mountain pass. "We are nearly over the saddle. What say you to crossing that point, and setting up camp on the downward slope?"

Warin agreed with me, a bit to my surprise since I thought we were still quarrelling. Nevertheless it was good to know that he would be practical even when we were facing disagreements. I shook my head. No sense in thinking like that. There was no 'us'. There was no need to be thinking about him being practical.

He was a man I'd met a long time ago, and now he was just my guardian, the same way that the brothers and Noble had been. The thought made my chest swell and my throat lock. I wanted something different from that, how I wanted a man who would be as a husband to me, but I would have to content myself with the knowledge that at least for now, I was safe.

Warin passed me up with his black horse and set to leading us down the trail. He was good, his experience on the roads showed, but he hadn't spent as long in these mountains as I had. For the remainder of the day we took turns finding the trail, but it was by far the fastest when it was me in the lead. An hour or two later we were climbing a steep trail, and I heard Richmond utter a curse and grumble.

They had to be hungry, even I was hungry, and I'd been sneaking nibbles of bread crusts, but this was no place to stop. Too steep, no room on the trail to even set up a fire ring, much less have place to sit down around it and cook. We would have to endure, just a half mile more, but I at least needed a distraction from the stinging in my arches and the nervous edge that waiting for a storm gave. Warin's horse paused, heaving, and I passed him by, motioning that Warin should wait to let Lord Richmond catch up to us while I went ahead and investigated the remainder of the trail.

As large and impressive as the horses were, their heads drooped and their hooves slipped as the sun dropped low in the clouds and the temperature grew colder, turning slush of midday into ice.

Richmond's horse slipped and scraped his legs when we were over the worst of the climb. I left The Mule at a tree and met the shaken lord and his horse as they limped up the trail. Though the bay favored his leg, I found nothing wrong with the joints when I felt his leg from hoof to chest, and the scrape was enough to bleed and that was it.

"He was raised on the plains, wasn't he?" I asked and shook my head.

Lord Richmond's cheeks were pink and his eyes tired, but my comment gave a gleam of life to his face. "How do you know? Are you so fine a judge of horse breeding?"

"She knows that any horse birthed in the mountains would make these slips as a foal, and not as an adult," said Warin.

I nodded. When the horse persisted in lamenting over his leg, I took a scrap of fabric from the pack and wrapped it while Warin went ahead to find a place to camp. Richmond watched me in silence and insisted he lead both animals to where Warin had a trail of smoke rising over the tree tops. Once there, Richmond and

Warin began to set up camp. They moved in a methodical routine, one I realized that I would be disrupting by trying to help. I went for water instead.

What water there was to find was old and murky, but the alternative was to melt snow, which always tasted dusty. After a moment of consideration, I filled the pot with the cleanest water I could, and dipped my bracelet into the water. Like fresh water cutting through muck, the bracelet purified the pot. I returned to camp, hiding my bracelet again and wondering if I should toss some snow into the pot, so it didn't taste suspiciously clean. I wasn't sure what they knew about me, but I didn't want to add to their concerns.

Dinner was a simple affair, dried pork boiled until it was soft and pliable enough to chew, served with hard bread from one of the packs. If anyone noticed the purity of the water past the salt cure from the pork, no one commented. We all had dull eyes from too long slugging through snow. Lord Richmond stood, taking his bowl with him, a blanket draped about his shoulders while his cloak dried in front of the fire, and stared out back the way we came. "We must have travelled twenty miles through poor conditions today."

Warin lifted his head from taking another bowl, leaving enough for another helping for Richmond and me. "I think it was nearer to twenty-two miles, if my memory serves me correctly."

Richmond watched as I rotated my shoes, seeing that I had tucked my toes beneath my body to warm them. "What is your guess for distance covered, Melody?"

"I think that people are too concerned at the rate of

their speed, when they should be focused more on arriving at their destination at all."

Richmond laughed and came to warm his fingers by the fire. "But an army which arrives too late does as much harm as an army which doesn't arrive at all."

"Then it is good I am not in the army."

The burly man across from me shook his head. "Nonsense. Had you been male and Warin of less dubious descent, you'd make sure our armies never arrived late, and never got lost."

I could have rankled at the clumsy compliment, much the same way Warin did with a lip twitch and brow furrow, but I knew there was something better to say. "If we were as you said, then we wouldn't have had the experiences which lead to us being competent pathfinders."

Richmond thought about that in silence.

I finished the pot, and the three of us looked at it, still hungry, while our animals cropped away on nearby grasses. It was as though we were each thinking about making more food, but weren't sure how much more we needed. Richmond finally made the decision and swooped into action as the world darkened without a definite sunset.

Night came all too quickly, and I was glad for Richmond's unexpected cooking abilities when he made a second meal, this one with onion and carrot and a bit of barley and salt pork. I thought that I hadn't eaten so well since I'd met the abbot, and my stomach bulged and my eyelids grew heavy. The man insisted on tossing three blankets upon me for sleeping, claiming that my cloak would be insufficient. He did not know that the unicorn fur would keep me warmer than any wool, but I accepted to avoid questions.

"We are followed," Warin said as Richmond fell to sleep.

I looked to where Warin pointed, and I saw a white creature advance upon our camp beneath the starlight, startling the heavy haze about my head into wakefulness. The horses slept as though nothing had changed, but The Mule woke now and then, seeming a little uneasy. Though I was tired, I no longer felt like I could sleep.

"Do you have something in mind?" I asked Warin.

"There is a rock fifty paces below. If the creature will come so close to camp, I will not be at ease resting."

Neither would I. But did this mean we were beyond our petty fighting? I studied Warin, my eyes drifting eventually to where he gripped a walking stick. Squinting, I realized now that it was no mere stick, but one that had been polished and carved, with runes scratched in a spiral down the staff. The dragons had spoken to me of such staves, and of the power wielded by the magicians who owned them. Was it a new acquisition, or did he have it when we'd first met? I couldn't remember. No matter when he'd gotten it, its presence made me feel more secure. With not another word, I stood back upon my feet and went down to the rock, taking with me the blankets to sit upon.

Once I was situated and warm, my eyes grew heavy again, even as my mind was disturbed with knowing that thing was down below. To keep myself from falling asleep, I sang and hummed softly, focusing on the chill of the night air and testing it, asking the air what the weather would hold in the day to come. For a time, I was silent, listening to the wind on my arms, and to the stillness around me. I focused on the way of the world, sensing the environment and letting it seep under my skin. I tasted dust on my tongue and felt wet upon my hand: More snow would come. Then there was the crunch of snow, and I opened my eyes.

Thirty paces downhill, a spiralled horn caught the light, and thick mane tossed in the wind. Heavy fog formed before the creature's nose and he breathed in deeply, taking three huffs of my scent on the breeze, leaning towards me as though he wished to advance, but not moving his feet. The unicorn knew. He knew I was a virgin. He knew I was days from no longer being one. He knew that a magician watched and waited.

And so the unicorn snorted and tossed his head, then looked my way again. I narrowed my eyes and tried to see better. Were his eyes blue? Was he the one who haunted my dreams and had hunted me for so long? If he were to come a little closer, then I would know for certain. But then he spun on his haunches and ran into the darkness, leaving us alone for the night.

Even though I hadn't seen his eyes, there was only one monster I knew which was as huge as him, and he was the only one who made such loud noise. Either he wasn't cautious, or he was too large to be as silent as the rest of his kind. After he had gone entirely from my sight, I returned to the fire, getting chilled in the short walk from my rock to the camp. Warin watched me as I folded myself as close as I could to the heat without burning myself. He said, "You have acted as a sacrifice before."

"It is not my desire," I replied, a little angrily, upset that he had realized this and that I had been so foolish as to give away my previous post. I should have fumbled, should have recalled the mistakes that I'd made when I was nothing but a child, but I had been too cold, too eager to draw the beast close so I could identify him. This was nothing I could blame on Warin, only myself. I needed to be more careful in the future.

"Why not?"

I shot him a glare for asking after a topic I didn't want to discuss. What would make him drop the subject? Nothing came to mind, at least not fast enough. The fatigue of the day had dampened my ability to think and banter back and forth with him. "I wanted something else."

"I think you will miss the fineries of such poaching," said Warin, his words clipped in irritation.

"I think you should keep your thoughts to yourself and let me keep mine. I have not shared more than my name and my talent, and I do not intend to." At my words, Warin raised an eyebrow and smiled, bringing a hot blush to my face as I crossed my arms in defiance. "Now allow me to sleep, unless *you* plan on doing so. In which case I will warn you that I am much too exhausted to remain on guard, no matter how vigilant I will try to be."

I turned away from him so I couldn't see the smug gloat on his face, even as I felt it lingering on my back and shoulders. The fire popped and hissed, and I nestled down in the blankets, trying to find sleep. Too late, I realized that by running away from the argument, I was surrendering victory to him with my silence. How could I cope with dragons and the dangers of the wilderness, yet not be able to control the conversation with one man? I hated it, yet I felt comforted by it as well. Warin let out a long breath, and I heard shuffling, then smelled pipe weed as it burned. He exhaled a long trail of smoke, I heard it and smelled it a second later, then he asked again, "Why did you leave your protectors?"

It was getting to be too much work to avoid answering him. And...I wanted someone to talk to. A peer, a companion, someone who knew the ways of the world that I did. Annoying as he could be, I didn't want to give that up for the sake of convenience. I propped myself up on my elbow, watching him make faces to make lopsided smoke rings. "I went to a naming ceremony for my friend's child. It was not the first I have attended, but it was the first time I knew...the first time I knew I wouldn't have one as well. It's not too late for me. But it soon could be. My entire life, I've been treated as a child."

When I thought about it, long-suppressed fury gave color to my cheeks and I hissed out so fast that it was a muddle of emotions rather than words, "The lies the women tell me! Of all the foolish things to meekly accept, of all the ridiculous tales I have heard. I knew their falsehoods, I'm too wise for the hunts now. I can do nothing for them except leave and hope I take that beast with me."

Warin shifted in surprise. "What are you speaking of?"

I pulled my cloak tighter about my shoulders, adjusted the blanket around my face so I could use it as a pad for my head. "I'm not going back, don't think you can force me."

"I wouldn't dream of it," Warin said, startled. Gazing back at him, I studied his eyes and found they were affectionate, protective, and afraid. Would he send me back? He said he wouldn't, and I believed him.

All of a sudden, I was frantic to not lose a confidant, no matter how little he deserved my secrets. "Don't tell anyone else. As I said, I'm worthless to the villages now."

"What are you talking about?"

I bit my tongue, warring between telling him everything and keeping myself safe. I looked to the fire and closed off my heart. "It's nonsense. I'm prone to nonsense. They've always told me so, particularly while I am tired. Have you anything else that needs done?"

Warin rubbed his forehead and let out a sigh. "No. You have done well today. Rest."

I turned my back to him and shut my eyes, but it was only when he began to sing a slow, rumbling travelling song that I fell asleep.

Snow weighed down on my chest, waking me when I stirred and some drifted to the back of my neck, then melted. I shrugged off the extra blankets and saw where Richmond had fallen asleep on guard while Warin rested. A quick survey of the camp showed that nothing had been noticeably bothered, and I didn't see any tracks in the fresh snow. Mindful to not wake them, I brought the fire back to life and heated up some food. We would need a hot meal and hot drink before we continued on the trail. It was still cold, and it would only get colder as the storm wandered through the sky.

When the scent of onion and oatmeal filled the camp, Warin emerged from his blankets and shrugged off the snow which had gathered upon him. Our trail had an inch of fresh powder over it, and the path behind us now looked positively unpassable, snow filling in holes in places where a slip would have been devastating even in the summer. Warin's lips hardened into a line, and I knew he was thinking that the climb down the other side would be just as treacherous. Caution needed to take precedence over speed. A stout stick would help to find the path, if we knew where to poke it.

Without disturbing Lord Richmond, I could only find one spoon, and I shared that spoon with Warin as we ate directly from the pot. It was hard to tell how much we'd eaten, but it must have been a good deal. Richmond joined us, rubbing his neck and grumbling. His gait was stiff and half his face was pinched in pain.

"Not another night on the road. Can't feel my ears. Or other things. Has everyone checked feet for frostbite?" He took the spoon, piled high with a steaming mass of thick porridge, and pointed it to a place where smoke billowed up from hills hiding a village. "It's a good distance, particularly in the snow. Once we're out of the worst of the trail, we will all ride. Anyone sight the beast?"

"It is not far, but it won't approach us while we are so near to Melody." The mage stepped away from the fire and began to pack everything; I decided it was best to stay out of his way and simply roll up blankets.

The two men continued in their planning, and as soon as Lord Richmond had finished his meal, I went to scrub the pot out with some snow. Not twenty paces from camp, next to currant bushes, were prints on top of the fresh snow. A man's boot print, and a large boot at that.

I measured it with my hand, finding it larger than even Richmond's bootprints. Another traveller? But I hadn't seen any sign that anyone had come up the path after us. There might be other trails, I conceded, but it didn't make me feel any more secure. Before we set out, I checked the area around camp for any sign of there being another person, or a fresh set of prints upon the trail. I only saw our own prints everywhere but where the man had stood watching us sleep. I shuddered at the thought, and fell into line. Best to leave this place behind.

It would not be so simple. The snow hid whole cliffs, and made the path seem to pass where it did not. Memory merged with sight, and I began to predict the trail. Every step forward was worthy of victory, but I did not celebrate, worried that my next step would be disaster. Even with me leading the way off the pass, the sun was in the center of the sky before we could take advantage of the horses.

"Ride behind me," Warin said.

By this point, I was panting, exhausted, and eager for a rest. I held out my hand; he slipped his boot out of the stirrup and I put my shoe in, swinging on the horse behind the saddle, grateful for the dry blanket I sat upon. As I resettled my cloak, it brushed by his arm and he hesitated, then stroked the lining.

"Hare?" he asked.

"It is soft," I said back, not willing to tell a complete lie. Warin said nothing.

It was dark when we reached a village in the hills, a place marked as much by the wood smoke as it was by the torches burning in the streets to keep fabled snow monsters at bay. Lord Richmond lead us to the widest street which ended in an inn at the crossroads of two streets. This inn was larger than the last, and more boisterous. Noble used to avoid it at all costs, but when I glanced down the other streets, I saw that the better inns were more than full, according to the red flags hanging by doors. It was here or the streets.

When Warin dismounted, I didn't think twice about following after him into a room so bright and so thick with pipe weed haze that my eyes watered. While the men made their bargains, I watched the activity before the hearth, this time there was a man with his hand down a woman's front, though he thought since he was in the back he could not be seen. They left to go to the privacy of a room, kissing as they went by me, bumping Warin and eliciting a growl from him.

Richmond paid for two rooms. The men shared a room, and I got the other. It was a simple place, four barren walls, one of which shared the chimney with a fireplace so heat and smoke entered my room. The bed was passable at best, but the bedding was fresh and nothing smelled poorly. I arranged my basket and hung my cloak to dry against the wall.

Someone knocked on my door. I opened it, cautiously,

then saw Warin. His face was hard. I wondered if he was tired, or upset over something. "We hunt tomorrow at first light. Sleep well, and be prepared to leave."

"I will." I didn't add that I was always prepared to leave. A chair propped under my door handle ensured I would sleep that night, a trick I'd learned from Noble. But what I didn't say—because Warin left suddenly— was that the storm wasn't over. It had only begun.

It was three days before a blizzard let up even enough for the village women to make it to their well without a rope tied about their waist, and even longer before the snow had melted to the point where we could ride out on the horses. The men looked caged, but I felt at ease. The storm that I had felt in my gut was here now, and we'd made it to safety. Hunting the beast would have to wait, and meanwhile I planned on making my presence here known.

By the second day, I had charmed a book out of an academic going home on suspension for fighting, and by the end of that night I had gazes following my usual routine: Reading, writing, and sewing by the fireplace, helping the innkeeper's wife clean tables from time to time, and eating meals with my protectors.

Warin had the sense to keep his gaze constantly upon me. Richmond soon claimed to be my father as a way to frighten off suitors, and it worked with those who had lower confidence or who were young men. Others wouldn't be frightened off by a snarl, but I took care to not entice them, merely be present. I had drawn the attention of the man who ran the livery, and he was keen to charm me. I considered letting him.

On the third day, Warin brought books out to my table and chased the men away. Though I had been anticipating the usual selection of 'goode works' suitable for any church-going woman, I found the books were on magic. If he intended for this to be an alternative way for me to pass my free time, it worked. When I asked him why he had given me that particular selection, Warin shrugged and said that it was what he had. Before long, I was so deeply entrenched in reading that I could only be bothered to leave my room for meals.

There came a knock on my door sometime during the fourth day, and I opened it absently, then returned to sit upon the bed. "Yes?"

"I'm glad to see I was neglected for a book, and not a thing which breathes." It was Gerald, the livery master, and he rested his elbow against the door frame. "May I come in?"

"No." I realized after I said it that the reply had been too blunt. "But you can stand there and talk if you would like."

"Would you be amendable to sitting before the hearth?"

My brow knit as I read something contradictory to how I understood the theory of magic. I shook my head. "I'm comfortable here."

"I'm comfortable where you are."

"Then you are at peace in your present position."

He chuckled. "What are you so involved in reading?"

I raised my gaze and gave the reply I always gave the

brothers. "Margaret's Prayer Book for the Honest Woman."

"Ah." Gerald's broad face was as blank as I had expected it to be. He was a fine-looking man, tall, muscular, free from unsightly deformities. It was a wonder he was unwed. A grin broke over his cheeks. "Find yourself needing a reminder to keep yourself from sinning around me?"

"Were you a more courageous man, I wouldn't hesitate to sin with you," I said, settling with my back against the wall and the book between my legs. I saw him stiffen.

"What makes you say such a thing?"

"You only came to see me when my guardians went away on their own business. You're avoiding them. Like a child. I want a man."

I heard the smile in his voice, even though I had my eyes down at my book. "Let me show you what a man is."

"I'd rather Warin show me," I said dismissively. While I said this, I realized it was true. Gerald was a toy. Perhaps a tool. Something to make Warin feel jealous. Any one of a hundred things could be said of that admission, and I couldn't deny the truth in that. It was what it was. I wanted Warin, and if I couldn't have him, I'd do my best to see him driven mad.

Gerald laughed. "He's half what I am."

"True," I said, "but he has courage twice that you do."

"You wound me," Gerald said, clutching his tunic over his heart. He wore as fine of fabric as ever I had seen, dark red with tablet weave around the neckline and cuffs. It was a heavy contrast to the slightly-felted gray wool hunting vest Warin wore.

I gave him a smile. "I am certain you would be braver under different circumstances. Supposing if there weren't two men to guard my virtue?"

"I would take an army for you, if we were on my home ground."

"Then I will be certain never to set foot in the livery," I joked.

His face faded from amused to serious, and he made a passing comment about leaving me to my prayers.

Long after he was gone, I stared at the wall in contemplation. Richmond found me tapping my finger against the book binding.

CHAPTER 16

Wind teased my hair as it hung in waves down my shoulders. I wore a gown the color of shadow upon the snow and the boots Richmond refused to let me remove. My cloak was nearby, as I had cast it off to enjoy the sun upon my body, though I knew that the lord would rather I wear that, too. He would have me so swaddled my scent would not carry to the great beast.

Now, as before, I wandered and sang, or from time to time I would read or pray. Richmond and Warin were not as good at following and staying hidden from the unicorn as Brother Jacob had been, so I felt tethered.

Snow drops and crocuses poked out from their white blanket, and I took my time gathering a bouquet of them, singing this time the mating call of several birds. Curious birds sang back to me. I could see the unicorn from time to time, but he remained distant. He might come to me during the dark of night.

In the late morning hours, I found myself wishing I'd brought a book to read while I instead wove a rough mat from stems of oats which had long been picked clean by birds. Once chill set into my bones, I walked again, mindful to remain out in the open. I didn't want the beast to find me in the same vulnerable position that the unicorn had on my first hunt.

The sun came out from behind clouds at midday, melted some snow, then hid behind gray storm clouds and eventually the land grew darker and darker, until the sky cleared to reveal a moon rising. No sign of the unicorn, but I knew he was out there, watching me. Hours after the stars came out, I saw Richmond motion for me. I sauntered towards him, picking the dried remains of berries along the way. Richmond was impatient when I at last reached him.

"It is time to retire for the night. We can try again in the morning."

"This is an old beast. He may lose interest if I am always coming and going. I can sleep in my cloak well enough." Even as I said this, though, I did feel tired and cold. Easter hunts weren't held in the winter so this was a challenge even for me, and I'd waded through more snow than was good for me.

Lord Richmond laughed, a noise that bounced off barren trees and made a squirrel shuffle in its burrow. "That may be, I am convinced you have dragon blood in your veins, but I haven't so much as a blanket. It is time to return."

If I did not agree to go back with him now, he would make so much noise as to frighten the beast away. So I mounted the black horse behind Warin, huddling close to his back for warmth, and enjoying it despite my efforts to not notice him. He took one of my hands, breathing life back into my fingers and rubbing them briskly. I thought that once or twice, when the moist heat of his breath was on my fingers, I felt the press of a kiss against my skin, but it might have been just from keeping steady on a horse who slipped on icy roads.

We were half way to the inn when I remembered something. "Everything and everyone has magic, yes?"

"To one extent or another." Warin didn't seem surprised that this was the first thing I'd said to him all day. Then again, little that I said or did surprised him.

"But some people are able to seize that magic and use it to meet their own purpose? And even take that magic from other people and things?"

"I did not think you were studying the books. I see I was mistaken."

Warin was very, very mistaken. Maybe I'd finally surprised him after all. I had been studying the books with fervor and admiration, many times having to take breaks to think about what the text said and contemplate its meaning. The most simple of terms were not explained, possibly because it presumed that the reader had a working knowledge of magic and a teacher who could discuss topics of confusion.

Technically, I had Warin to speak with, but our opportunities to talk were limited to these rides to and from the hunting fields. The innkeeper didn't like hearing talk of magic, no matter how carefully we guarded our words, and Warin seemed hesitant to divulge information, besides. I sighed. "Am I correct or not?"

"Yes."

I shivered, feeling tired from the day and annoyed by knowing that soon, the two of us would go into our separate rooms. Even sitting beside him in front of the fire was preferable to hunched up in bed with a heavy tome in my lap. "I am trying to understand. Help me."

"You are fine."

Was that a trickle of laughter coming through his voice? The thought made my heart still and my head swim. No time for that, I corrected myself. Focus on what I can count on. "So, anyone can at any time strip magic from other sources, *but* it is better and easier to accomplish when the source's natural defenses are hampered. Can you explain that to me?"

Warin chuckled, and the horse misstepped. I patted the horse's rump.

"Shall we take the humble turnip as an example? Admittedly, it has less power than other things, but it is a serviceable item for this purpose. Its power is the same in the ground as it is in the stew, but in the stew it is easy to consume because it has been pulled out of the dirt, washed, cut, and cooked. We may think in all things in this way. Perhaps not stones. It is no easy matter to eat a stone, but some may be mined, polished, and shaped for jewellery."

"And what of people?"

"What of them?"

"Warin," I let out a sigh. The horse took several more strides. If I did not have my answers soon, we would be back in the village and he would cease discussing it altogether. "How does a person get power from another person?"

A few dozen strides passed, and I thought he wouldn't answer me. Then he said, "Bargains. Tricks. Gifts.

Services. Time spent in each others company. Often the power is a reciprocal movement, one borrowing from the other until it is paid back. But...for other purposes, there are rituals and words which may strip a person of power. It is more difficult to do this when the intended target is in a strong position or supported by other people. However, a target may be placed in a new environment where they know no one to loan them strength. It is easiest to take power from a stranger in your home."

"And the stage of their life matters, too? Richmond would be a difficult target, at the height of his strength and age and skill. But in another twenty years, perhaps less..."

"...he will be struggling to compensate for slower reaction time and impaired senses, and will be uncomfortable in his own body. You are correct again. Transition phases make a target weak."

Then we were passing houses puffing with smoke and billowing with talk and laughter, and our conversation came to a halt.

One day bled into the next, and days became weeks which became months. The air grew colder, and I grew stubborner. The creature knew the range of Warin's magic and Richmond's bow, and he remained just outside of it, though he spent long hours staring at me from the shelter of the woods, knowing I could see him and he could see me.

"If he is not causing harm, we should let him be, Warin," said Richmond one evening while we warmed our feet before the fire. We were one of the few guests, the others having moved on while we had remained to hunt the unicorn.

"If he was a nuisance before, he will be more of one now," Warin said, shaking his head. "Unless you plan on telling five fathers that their daughters died for naught."

"You used others to bait him before?" I asked. They hadn't mentioned this in the past, and from the way Lord Richmond wiped his hand over his brow, he didn't want to remember the earlier victims.

"*He* found *them*, and all of them within help of the house. If they had cried out."

I knew why they hadn't. What girl would, upon seeing a unicorn for the first time? I frowned.

"Did you see the draw?" I asked, remembering something. "If someone can get on top of the ridge, I will hide below them and wait for the beast to approach."

"How do you know he will?" asked Richmond, skeptical because someone would have to cross a frozen river.

"He wants me. He will come."

"If he wanted you, we would have him already," Warin said.

A chill breeze announced Gerald entering the inn, stopping me from saying that the unicorn was biding his time. Gerald crossed to the innkeeper to place an order, he preferred a strong honey mead, and I didn't feel like speaking with the stablemaster today, no matter how briefly.

I stood and told Warin, "If you want to leave, then by all means *do*."

I strode back to my room then sat upon my bed, playing absentmindedly with a head wrap I had been embroidering for the innkeeper's wife. It was warm and private here, like a tiny house all to myself, complete with a wooden chair and an oatgrass mat in the center of the floor. Odd how this inn had become more of a home to me than the brother's cottage ever had been.

There came a knock upon my door, and Warin looked in without waiting for an answer. "What was that about?"

Chin high, I stared at him and gave no reply. He stepped inside.

"Go away."

Instead he sat down on the bed next to me. I had to look away to hide a smile.

"Not until you explain yourself."

Facing him, I examined him from wind worn brown hair to the way he leaned on one arm. My knees brushed his. Hand shaking in spite of myself, I touched his cheekbone, stroking his beard with my thumb. For an instant, I wondered if he would pull away. My heart thudded in my ears and my mouth went dry.

Then he reached up, cupping his hand over mine, pressing my skin firmer against his own. I felt muscles relax as a long breath left his lips. His eyes closed and I saw his breathing become shallow. My stomach twisted as I debated what I should do, knowing that he wouldn't take the lead. Did he want it, like I did? I didn't know. I couldn't know. Kiss or no kiss, I could make a mistake both ways. Better to regret what I had done than what I hadn't.

I kissed him.

His lips were warm and chapped, soft and sharp. A low sound, like a groan, rumbled in his throat, sending warmth through my body and heating even my cold fingers. My nose bumped his cheek and I began to pull back, embarrassed at my own clumsiness but thrilled with the results nevertheless.

A calloused hand cupped my face. I let him draw me back to him, and tried to relax my nerves as he taught me how to kiss. It started slow, a gentle pressure of soft lips, rough cheeks, wandering fingers, and uncombed hair. Then there was the hot dash of a tongue on my lips, and soon the gentle pressure gave way to hard kisses, tongues dancing, and a quick lesson on avoiding the clashing of teeth. I could have let my embarrassment over a tight jaw overtake the situation, but I was too pleased with my accomplishment. Warin, despite his aloof tendencies and proclamations otherwise, felt the same ache for me as I did for him. It was what I'd wanted to know.

My breath came in gasps when I pressed on his chest and pushed him away. Reluctantly, he allowed me to put distance between us. Cheeks flushed, I giggled at the hunger I saw in his eyes. It was a similar hunger to the one that had been in Judas' eyes, but different. This was a caring hunger, one that made the lines in his face soft. There was no intimidation in his gaze, just invitation. It was so similar, yet so very different.

"He will come," I whispered, "for the same reason you did."

Warin swallowed and tried to clear his head. "We aren't alike at all."

"No," I agreed, "but you want the same thing, yet very different things as well."

Warin did not know what to say to that. It was hard to explain. I didn't know if it made sense, or if I understood it, either. I slipped into his arms, put my head to his chest, and listened to his heart.

"Are you doing this out of fealty to your lord?" Warin asked.

"No."

"Then why not leave while you can?"

"What, in the dead of winter?"

He sighed. "While your own lord thinks success is impossible."

I paused, wondering for a minute if I should tell him. "I have spent my entire life being hunted. I am going to put an end to that."

While we made our way to the ravine, I looked for signs of unicorn. I found only snow drops in the places I would expect to find it, not indicating that a unicorn had been even in the area for some time. The beast was unlike anything I had ever encountered. It was why I feared the unicorn so. It was also why I was so determined to face it.

At first, worry ate at my stomach and I worked a tear in my dress until I realized I was making it larger. I set about reading, but couldn't focus. The sun took its time crossing the sky, and when my breath fogged before my mouth and the light darkened with the press of storm clouds, I was heavy with disappointment. I had been so certain the beast would come today.

I signalled the end of the hunt by standing up and waving.

Richmond and I went to join Warin, and I crossed the river first, feeling out the ice, showing Richmond the path. It was good, solid ice stemming from a prolonged deep freeze. Richmond began to follow in my steps as Warin greeted me with, "We will try again."

I scowled and went to where we had hidden the horses.

The Mule twitched his ears all around and let out a loud bray. I opened my mouth to yell back at him, but a tingling sensation across the back of my neck stopped me.

A shriek, like the wail of a banshee mixed with the squeal of an angry horse, pierced the woods. Cutting between me and where Warin helped Richmond cross the ice, a white monster hurdled a fallen tree towards the mage, his horn lowered. It seemed to have grown even larger since I had last seen it, thicker through the chest and legs with muscle owed to his pursuit.

It snorted and tossed its head once, its mane cleared from its eyes. Fear knotted in my gut as the unicorn slid to make the corner and thundered at Warin, his hands just beginning a spell. I worried he had no time.

Yelling, I found carrots in the saddle bag, and ran into the fray, throwing carrots and numbly noticing their color as a yellow fell short, a purple struck the rump, and a white hit his ear. The monster turned his head to glare at me with one eye, but did not falter in his stride. Warin dodged to the side and released a ball of fire. Flames rolled over the beast's neck, but only curled hair. The unicorn pivoted on a hoof and slipped, but not enough to take it down, just enough to raise small furls of ice beneath black hooves.

He charged again.

An arrow sliced its shoulder and buried itself in a snow bank beside my knee. Rearing, the unicorn let out another cry, and his hooves slammed into the ice with a crack that reverberated through the ice and off the ravine. As he ran by Warin, he shoved the man with his shoulder, then kicked as the man fell.

"Warin!" I yelled.

The unicorn faltered and looked to me, then saw Richmond kneeling with another arrow notched. The beast's nose flared and he snorted, and ran off into the woods.

"The ice," I said, snapping out of shock. "Get off the ice!"

My hands were fast with the rope as I tied one end into a loop and tossed it to Richmond. He was crawling across the river, and his sleeves were dripping as he moved to where Warin was huddled in a ball. Worry for how broken he was made my hands fumble as I anchored the rope to a tree, just in case.

"Here!" I tossed Richmond a blanket. He rolled Warin onto it and began to pull.

I threw him a second rope. "Tie it to the blanket and move away, there's too much weight."

While Richmond inched away, I began to pull Warin. Richmond followed after him. The ice cracked over and over again, making *booms* that stopped my heart and made my sweat run cold.

It was seconds and ages before my fingers touched

Warin's blanket, and I pulled him to safety. I touched his head, and his eyes focused on mine, but he was clutching his ribs. No coughing up blood, though. I returned to the shore.

Richmond was ten feet from safety when he disappeared.

I didn't yell when a fresh rush of heat pulsed through my veins. I hauled on the rope. It was all slack at first, and I found myself panting and yanking the rope, frantic. Then my hand met resistance like a rock, and I heaved myself against it while sweat turned to ice down my back and I seemed to make no progress.

There was nothing where once there had been Richmond. Now it was water freezing over the surface, coming up in thin sheets when the rope twitched.

Richmond's hand burst into the air. I dragged myself against the rope, whistled for The Mule. My feet were being pulled through the snow, leaving bare the frozen ground in gouges behind me.

A warm nose bumped my back. Never in my life had I been so happy to see the droopy mule. Richmond lunged and swung his arms onto a ledge. I took the slack and tied it to The Mule's pack saddle. My fingers were numb and worked clumsily. No sooner did The Mule feel the tug of the line then his ears went back and he grunted.

We pulled together. Three more times Richmond broke through the ice into the river, until he was in the shallows which were frozen thick, and we pulled him to the shore.

Richmond shivered as he cast a frightened glance at the sky. "Fire. We need fire. Warin. How is Warin?"

Richmond looked close to joining him in oblivion. I ran to my basket, and pulled out a dragon scale the size of a shallow serving bowl.

I sang to it, getting the tone wrong first in my panic, then dropping my voice and focusing on the sounds the dragons had taught me. It responded as I relaxed, beginning to glow stronger and stronger until the snow beneath and around it turned from ice to vapor, and leaves beneath it burned to cinders. The heat from it swelled to be like a blacksmith's forge on a hot day, and soon not even I could look upon it. I set up a line between the trees around us, and draped blankets on all sides to cut down on the draft.

Richmond dried his clothes and tended to Warin. I made a hot infusion from dried mint. When Warin awoke, he looked to me and the dragon scale, and spoke a few words with Richmond. They said nothing to me. It was just as well. I was occupied singing a dragon song, almost humming it as I remembered the dragon who had given it to me.

The inn was a steady stream of fussing when we arrived just before dawn, alive but cold. The two men had spent the entire ride talking in whispers, and I had spent it picking out a path through freshly fallen snow. I didn't know what they had said, but Richmond watched me, worn and wary, the way a shepherd watches a traveller passing by the flock.

At Richmond's resounding order, the innkeeper left us alone at a fully stoked hearth. Richmond had his shoulder to me at all times, and seemed larger and more intimidating than he usually was. He wouldn't respond to my attempts at conversation.

Finally, he said, "I do not know what to say to you or what to think. Are you my loyal servant or are you a traitor?"

He went back to staring at the flames. I didn't understand, but I worried that he knew where it was I came from. He knew I left my post. But how? And why now, of all times?

It was only when Warin spoke that I began to understand. "The gryphon claw. The unicorn bracelet. Your cloak. Now the scale. Only a scale taken from a living dragon could have that much power, and only a person working with a sorcerer could know the words to its magic. You are a poacher, and you're using us to get that great unicorn."

I stared at him, uncomprehending at first. He continued, "What happens to your companions? Do you kill them after they come to trust you?"

Now I closed my eyes and sighed. Which was worse, to have them think this of me, or to let them know the truth? I buried my head in my hands and muttered, so softly I hoped they wouldn't hear, "I'm the virgin."

Stunned silence met this, then Warin laughed in mirth. "I suppose you would *have* to be. Did the role get tiresome and so you struck out on your own?"

He still thought I was part of the poachers. "*No.* You don't understand. I'm not *a* virgin, I'm *the* virgin."

I refused to look up to see if the message was getting through. My cheeks burned. I couldn't believe I was confessing to being a traitor, after all. When no word came, I said, "You see, I never left Brother Jacob after I met you. I'm the girl who goes in Lord Richmond's name to tame the dragons. I'm the one Brother Jacob follows for the Easter hunt."

Richmond's boots scraped on the floor when he faced me. I still wouldn't look up.

"I was nine when I went to my first dragon. Ragnark. He was dying. He gave me his tooth. The dragons, they talk to me, they share their knowledge. Do you know what it is to be treated with respect by the most ancient and powerful of creatures, then go to a place where people whisper behind your back and even the children make jokes you don't understand? To be humiliated one way after another, and find solace only in the quiet of the woods?" Nails dug into my fist as I steadied myself to say, "I regret to inform you, milord, that I am both your most noble servant, and a most heinous traitor. I left my post."

No one knew what to say to me, not even three days later.

We waited for Warin to recover, but he only declined, growing pale and weak upon his feet. The magic laughing in his eyes was slowly leaving him. It hurt me more to watch him than it hurt him to experience.

After a sleepless night, I walked to Richmond, saw him checking on Warin. Richmond nodded in silent greeting.

I said, "The ice did not just crack. That was a spell. Not the kind that Warin does. It was something of the natural world, but I don't know precisely what, or how it works. Every race has its own magic, and I've seen enough of dragon and unicorn to know those well.

Perhaps the unicorn is working with a sorcerer, or was raised by one. It is impossible to say."

Richmond shook his head at me. "I know a spell, too. And I know when the only thing left to do is hope and pray."

I bit back a reply. There was more I could do. There had to be more.

"I love him," I whispered. "And he's dying."

Richmond looked down to Warin, then turned sad eyes to me. He put a hand on my shoulder, but had no other comfort to offer.

My eyes lit upon Warin's books, and I remembered the night I had kissed him. I remembered our conversation. I left before it was too late.

CHAPTER 17

Horse sweat and leather greeted me upon entering the livery. I yelled, "Gerald!"

I'd wanted to use my charms to borrow a horse from him, but I had only to look up and down the isle to see that the livery was empty. Even the stable boy was gone. That was very unusual, as though he had gone in advance of me. The Mule swung his head over the door and flicked his ears at me, but I was suddenly too impatient to saddle a horse.

With nothing more than a frown, I adjusted the basket on my shoulder and set out on the road on my own two feet. The urgency to hurry wasn't something that I consciously knew, it was something in the air that I felt, sinking its teeth of anxiety deep into my gut. I needed to do this, now. There was an order to it, but I didn't know what I was doing or why. I followed my instincts. I followed my territory. I followed the subtle signals in the air and land and water.

Beyond the last squat house I walked, beyond the frozen river and the tree the children liked to play in, beyond the hills and into the forest I travelled. Where the woods were quiet with bated breath and a crop of snow drops overtook the white of snow banks, I stopped and took a slow turn in the meadow.

"Come get me," I whispered, my voice breaking the spell of silence upon the land. "Come claim me."

Nothing seemed to have heard me, yet everything had. No blackbirds were in the trees, nor were there hares on the ground or even the babble of a creek. Oh, this place had heard me, and the summons had gone out. All I needed was to wait for them to bring him to me, the same way my father waited for a sick lamb to step forward from the flock. The silence wrapped around me, completely enveloping the forest so thoroughly that I could have heard a child crying in the village.

Except no child cried. There was no noise, nothing except for the slow plodding of hooves crashing their way through the forest, making their steady way to where I stood, arms out from my body, waiting, calling him to a challenge in which one of us would lay claim to everything that the other had. I knew this. The beast had to know it, as well. If he didn't, he was a fool.

The crashing came to a stop and even the breeze dropped off, so the only motion in the glen was the tug and push of air in my lungs. When I next looked behind me, the unicorn stood there, watching me with cold fire in those blue eyes. His horn was lowered at my chest, and his ears rotated as he listened for hunters.

"I am alone," I said, "and still pure."

Stepping high, he circled me, and I faced him with an outstretched hand.

"Smell me. Touch me."

His ears flattened and he shook his mane. He snorted and ground his teeth.

I crossed my arms and stepped back. "Very well. If you won't have me, I will go to one who will."

As though insulted, he bolted forward and cut me off, lowering his horn and bringing it within a few inches of my heart. I set my jaw and stood rigid. Taking a deep breath of my scent, the unicorn's nostrils flared and his chest inflated. His lip curled back over his nose. Then he tossed his mane and relaxed, swishing his tongue. His ears pricked forward and he nickered.

Then his eyes laughed at me and he faced me with his side, tossing his head at his withers as though to prompt me to mount.

"If I come, I want you to release Warin from whatever spell is upon him."

The unicorn snorted, nostrils flared, spittle landing on my dress. He threw his head back and bellowed a shrieking noise that sounded like laughter.

I felt the change, the slight shift in the wind, the hair on my arms rising, the way my heart stopped, before I saw anything morph. The woods darkened and for a few seconds, only a slant of light illuminated the meadow, hitting at odd angles on the skin of the beast. Silver gleamed off the unicorn's withers, his horn flashed, and he drew up onto his back legs, hooves pawing at the sky.

The shriek changed, growing deeper, raspier, transforming into a laugh that sounded like dragon tail scraping on stone. The horn disappeared. Hooves turned to hands. The body shrank, but not enough. The form that took shape before me was human, but a large one, like a giant. Broad shoulders, massive hands, a stature which towered over mine.

The hide of a gryphon hung over his shoulders, worn like a cape, and he wore a breastplate made of black dragon scale. His sword was a unicorn horn carved to double-edges. When I took a breath to steady my nerves, I caught his scent, like rotten potatoes and fresh blood. Despite myself, I staggered back. He grinned, his teeth stained.

"Tell me, girl, what good is it to me if you agree to a walk with me? You and I have shared quite the courtship," He said.

"If you want my maidenhead, what has stopped you from simply taking it? Why all this?"

"A forced virgin is still virgin." He paused, considering. "If you were a common girl, I could marry you and you would have to consent. But you have no father to tell you that you must do so. So you see, I may not force you, and my attempts to woo my way under your skirts have proven to be less than productive."

I shot him a glare. "What attempts? As a unicorn?"

Then he bowed his head, and I saw him undergo another transformation, this one more subtle, just a shrinking of his frame and a rearrangement of his features. He looked up, and it was a familiar face.

"Gerald!"

Gerald lit a blue ball of light over a palm and studied it. "You understand, I had to keep a careful eye on my prize to see to it that no other man took what was mine. I had hoped for a quiet romance, but here we are. I believe you have come to strike a bargain?"

I swallowed, took a deep breath, and focused on the challenge. "Which would be what?"

The blue ball wove between his fingers. "Your virginity for his life. I won't force you, though...with the circumstances as they are, how about we consider this an exchange? One gift for another?"

I rankled at the thought and hissed, "You'd make a whore of me?"

"No, you would make one of yourself. If you aren't one already."

"What do you mean?"

Gerald shrugged. "You have been using your body to buy peace and meat. Have you not?"

The thought that the brothers had made a whore of me! I shuddered, crossed my arms. I had been expecting Gerald' demands, but those words...those words I had not anticipated. I resisted the urge to scowl. Instead I said, "If you do not wish a walk with me, what is it you do wish?"

The man darted his eyes down my frame. I stood before him, unflustered. He said, "The same I wanted of everything else. To consume you."

A chill ran down my spine. I looked at the dragon breast plate. "You *ate* them? The things you wear as trophies?"

The sorcerer shook his head. "No. Eating means chewing and swallowing. I *consumed* them. I took their magic. I took the best they had. Everything they were resides within me."

My head swirled. What demonic powers did this give the man who stole what he was unable to wield?

"How did you kill the unicorn without a sacrifice?" I was not sure why this question came out of my lips when there were so many others which might have done better.

The sorcerer gave a startled laugh. "You helped me."

"Me?"

"I was there on your hunt. A unicorn almost beat me. Don't you remember?"

I clutched my head and tried to not feel sick. This man, this *thing*, had come to me in the shape of a unicorn, and...and...it was too horrifying to think about.

"Ah, yes, you do remember me quite fondly. What charming roses in your cheeks, my sweet. See, I had intended to have you both, but unicorns are ever so powerful." The man inhaled deeply, as though he smelled a roast on the fire, and gave me a smile. "Which reminds me of your request, my virgin. See, nothing, not dragons, not unicorns, not harpies or sirens or gryphons or kings or magicians, are safe from my grasp. But a virgin can bring them to lay down their arms and render the beasts submissive for slaughter. I cannot."

I knew, somehow, that when the sorcerer was done with me, he would seek out Warin and Richmond, and take what was theirs for his own. He would be rising to the height of his power, and he would want territory and to strip the land of whatever he pleased. And since I had hunted so many more unicorns than him and tamed every dragon within a week's ride of here, I was the most powerful thing in the land, and I was its last defense. This soothed me more than thinking of the one man I wanted desperately to recover.

"You are quiet, my dear Melody, do tell me what is

upon your mind?"

"Only that there are so many virgins to select from," I said, staring at him calmly. "Why do you honor me so with your prolonged pursuit?"

The rumble which left his lips was a laugh I had heard throughout my life, yet never from a man. "I have been looking some time for a worthy woman. You see, a virgin is a fine delicacy. It must be trained properly, shaped well through life, and aged to the cusp of blooming."

A fresh chill ran through my body. He spoke of me as though I were a wine or cheese. To him, I likely was. "Why? No, I know that you want my power. But *how*? How does one take the power of a virgin?"

Eyes drifted down my body in the way that I had caught Warin watching me when he thought I did not see. But the feeling this man evoked was chilling. "I should think that would be obvious."

"Not to me."

"Surely you cannot be so pure as to not know the answer?" His tone was mocking.

"If I were not so pure, could I have so thoroughly lured you?"

The man did not have an answer to this.

I dipped my head and moved towards the underbrush. Pausing by a tree, I called back to him, "Come get me then. If you are so mighty you will catch me easily."

The man's brows furrowed. He said, "And if I do?"

My fingers caught on rough bark as I stepped onto a hare path. I called after, "We are creatures of the wild. What do they chase for?"

And then, while he pondered my meaning, I tapped

him lightly on the shoulder and ran, singing a tune as I went. A few steps away, I turned and taunted him. He wasn't letting me get away so easily, was he? The sorcerer laughed behind me, confident in his eventual success.

Though I had a destination, I disguised it by following the curves of the earth, running through the forest with the sure gait of a local. Thickets had grown in on certain areas, but the stags and does had changed their habits around the obstacles, which I followed. Gerald took the game with a deal of joy, using his magic merely to keep his breathing even and his body strong. At least, that was at first.

When I showed no sign of slowing down, he drew up boulders from the ground to block my path. I climbed them, even when my shaking hands caused me to slip. We were nearly there. Perhaps I'd been mistaken in not taking a more direct route. He made the branches reach for my hair and dress. I pushed through them, going slower now, lungs aching but still moving. I wanted to stop, but would not allow that of myself. I could see the hill now. When we were so deep into the forest that the land would not respond to him, he turned into a winged beast and flew overhead. He lit the forest on fire, ringing me in a circle.

I covered my mouth and ran through the smoke and over the flames, glad for my encounters with dragons. No sooner had I broken those ranks than the fires died down. Gerald was not behind me, but I wasn't sure where that meant he was.

I entered a glen and ran to a stream with flowing

water, taking a moment to drink from it. Then I jogged up a slope, slipping every now and then. Exhaustion made my limbs slow and the hill steeper than ever. I peered around a bush, looking for Gerald. I had not seen him in some time.

Arms grabbed my waist, and a breathy voice whispered, "If you want to get away, you should stop humming."

I did, but not because he suggested it. The song was over, and now I was unsure of what would happen next.

I smiled, took his arm. I panted, "Take me to the top."

The sorcerer picked me up and carried me, apparently liking the idea of the top of the hill better than the side. He grunted and heaved as he trudged up the slope. Once at the top, I slid to the ground and teased him to dance.

"No more games," he growled and took my arms.

He threw me upon the grass, his eyes blazing with an unnatural gleam. I laughed at him. "Are you not man enough to take me as you are naturally? Or do you need magic for a man's duty?"

Gerald smirked, then cast off his dragon scale armor, his gryphon cloak, his unicorn sword. The magic left his eyes and he stood before me naked. He said, "Is this man enough for you?"

I wasn't sure what to expect at this point. My confidence faltered when he knelt before me and spread my legs. He leaned forward, covering me. Horror set in as I realized how very small I was as he kissed me, his mouth hard, in between soothing words I didn't listen to and wouldn't have believed. I suddenly doubted. What had I done? But there was no backing down now. Warin's life depended on me. I kissed him, ran my hand down his ribs, then reached between us, Ragnark's claw in my hand.

I found the spot where his ribcage ended, and I thrust the dragon claw into his skin. I watched as it grew upon striking blood, piercing him through his chest. It took a second for him to open his eyes and stare at the protrusion. The blade shattered. He went a little white. Shock faded from his gaze and triumph filled his eyes.

Blood upon his lips, he let out a breathy laugh. "I've had worse."

Gerald reached up and touched the wound, and I felt magic rise as he said, "Heal."

But the magic did not go to him. It could not go to him. He looked confused, stared at the red on his hands, and tried again. "*Heal.*"

The smile on my lips was one of sympathy. I wished that I hadn't been forced to confront him, but it was my duty. Only now that he was staring at me, completely pale, trembling with shock and terror, did he realize what had happened. I cared for the king's land and people, the way my father cared for his land and livestock. I didn't tend to a meadow or a road, I knew now what my fortune had known all along: I watched after the mythical creatures and the mages. I was here to keep the balance of the good and evil. Gerald might be my first sorcerer, but he wouldn't be the last.

I soothed him as he died. With his last breath, his magic and all that he had destroyed and collected hung in the air, watching and waiting, still bound to this place by his flesh. I sealed his wounds, then cleaned the blood from our bodies.

Then the sorcerer's body shrivelled, becoming smaller and smaller and drier and drier, then turning to dust. When the wind came again, it took his body with it. I stared after the ashes, gazing at the wind long after all traces of the man were gone.

I had known he wouldn't give back Warin's life. Ragnark had ensured with his dying breath that I would understand what was told to me. I hobbled to the spot where the hill began, a smaller ridge. I put my hand on what had been Ragnark's head.

Never attack a mage on his home ground. Particularly not in his home, and especially not where he has buried his dead.

I closed my eyes and let the rhythm of the forest sing through my body. I released the soul of the black dragon, of the unicorn, of the gryphon, and of nearly a hundred others, feeling the world thicken as they found homes in the elements. I breathed easily again, and I looked in the direction of the town, and I saw where Warin hunched over his horse, coming for me, lead by The Mule.

I met him on the flat of the glen.

"Melody," he said. He looked haggard and pale and cold, but his eyes had the spark of magic in them.

"Warin. Gerald's dead. He was the sorcerer and the unicorn."

"All I care is that you live," Warin said, half-dismounting half-falling off his horse. He took me into his arms, and I kissed him until the world spun and then fell away, leaving the two of us in a hazy landscape of utter bliss. We collapsed together and made love under the rising sun.

Read on for an exclusive excerpt from
SWAN QUEEN

I

A sign winked in the wind, a painting of an adolescent swan beating her wings, her eyelids heavy with lashes and exaggerated liner as she gazed at those admiring her derrière, a suggestive illustration which I might have taken offense to, had the artist made it during my lifetime. Possibly it dated as far back as my grandmother's time, but I thought it more likely to be from when my mother had taken reign. Even illiterate, the peasants knew how to express themselves.

So this was to be where the villagers wanted to gather for a guild meeting? Were they mocking me, or merely testing my resolve?

"We should demand a change of venue, Katarine," said Luke, scowling at the tavern's sign, his boots digging to gravel of streets strewn with leafy hay which fell out of carts heading to barn lofts.

The Sable Swan hunkered down like a Southern cottage, a long, low tavern with stalls around the back, unlike the inns around the keep which were built on tall stilts to avoid flood waters. And to better hide from armies. I mused that in a country torn by war, this tiny village seemed to think that there were no Southerners, that there wasn't a strained ceasefire waiting to break. That there was just this country, this want for matters to be resolved at home. My brother could live for the war. I'd live for this.

But I was still staring at the sign, noting something for the first time. "They didn't use any writing."

I glanced back the way we came, to the squat houses hiding behind stalls of grain kernels—wheat, rye, quinoa seeds—and squash so fresh from gardens that clay loam fell off courgettes and onto the tables. When I remembered bushels of pears taking over the space where berries usually resided, I realized both that the children had been putting up hay yesterday and that they would never see a tutor in their life.

Luke' jaw slackened. "They can't read." Then it tightened again and he muttered, "Not that it stops them from making commentary."

"I know that," I said, ignoring his addition. Beside us came the steady *shhh, ssshhh, shhh* of a dressmaker cutting a skirt in the morning sun, one with narrower fullness and a shorter length than was customary. No new bolts of fabric graced her windows since I'd visited in the spring, a reminder that no matter how insulated this pocket of a village was, even it endured the shortages of war. "But that's not my point. I want to raise up a country of business. They're smart enough, so why not give them better tools? Arithmetic, and the ability to read and write a contract?"

Only here, nestled in the nook of a meadow between a creek and a forest, so far from anything of importance, was I allowed to wander the streets without the whole guard, taking with me just Luke. I had wanted to take Hanna with us, but that would signal the court that I didn't want to be alone with Luke, and any degree of weakness would spur gossip.

Luke shook his head. "Your mother would evict you from the keep if she heard such talk. It's not feasible to establish a monastery in every village."

What sort of a fool did he take me for? A monastery would take too much stone, and far, far too many years to build. "I'm not talking of a monastery in every village. Only a teacher and a quiet room."

"They might not want it. And where are you going to find these teachers?"

He did have a point; they might not want to change their ways any more than the court did, but how was I to know this unless I first gave them the option to choose a different path than the one they'd been born into? However, Luke's second question seemed ridiculous. "They'll be locals. The village will send a teacher and assistant to the keep to receive training. Villagers supply a living allowance so the villages will be committed to take their teacher and education seriously. While undergoing training, the teachers will room in our keep, of course, to prevent a housing strain."

Even now, Luke's eyes wandered uphill, to Ivy Lane, to the bakery where we used to share a kettle of anise and willow tea, and steaming bread slices smeared with apricot jam and soft farmer's cheese. Annoyed by his subtle request and by the prick of unbidden tears, I leaned toward the tavern with its scandalous opinion of my mother.

Luke stepped in front of me, barring entry. "You just thought of that when you saw the sign?"

Anything to keep me from changing the old ways, Luke? I wondered and took control of my emotions again. "No, I thought of it when you asked for a change of venue, which made me think you wanted a classier establishment, which made me wonder what one of the main pillars of class was, which brought me to education, which brought me to writing, and you know the rest."

Luke shook his head, but it wasn't in wonder. It was in refusal. "It won't work."

"It's a self-sustaining idea, with voluntary involvement. Why wouldn't it work?" And why did I sound like I was bickering?

Luke' eyes darkened at the terse quality of my tone, warning me against making a display, even here where I felt the greatest privacy. He said, "The money isn't the problem."

A loose strand came free from its coif and waggled before my eyes like a loose feather on my wing. I tucked my hair behind my ear and thought of the Queen in her reception hall discussing ore prices with her advisers. "No, it isn't."

The dressmaker lifted and shook out her pattern piece, drawing Luke's attention with a jerk. I walked toward the tavern, shocking Luke into objecting with a whispered, "Princess Katarine."

A dusty shepherd with a twisted leg and worn cane paused, recognizing me in an instant, and then held the door open for me. I lifted my chin and inquired over my shoulder, "Is there something amiss, Luke?"

He said, "No, Milady."

He wouldn't meet my gaze. My pose probably resembled that of the swan on the sign. Good.

I entered the Sable Swan, greeted first by dim lights and the pollen of fields, then the sweet yeasty scent of apples in the early stages of cidering.

Not enough candles made the sun draw vertical slits through closed shutters, providing a slitted view of long tables and wood chairs, and the distant hint of a mantle against the back wall. In a place without sconces or chandeliers, the tavern depended on open shutters for illumination. Many places did, but it was costly, and I wondered how much the tavern paid the local tax man to turn a blind eye to the window tax. Down the center of the tavern, tables were pulled together and surrounded by people of all ages drinking ales and cider, and eating hunks off a spit-roasted lamb leg.

Luke went tense, head not moving but I knew he was counting the burly men taking a rest from their fields. My own count suggested there were fifteen workers, and twice that in women and children. No wonder Luke stiffened. He was outnumbered.

The barkeeper, a short man with a missing arm and shiny head, jumped when he saw me. "Your highness! Princess Katarine! I was not expecting, please, I thought it was a jest, I will get my best..."

He must have thought it was at least plausible, or else he wouldn't have bothered to close up the windows.

"Barkeep," I said in a serious tone. "I would take a mug of ale, if you would be so kind. And open those shutters. If you have them you might as well use them."

I sat in the middle of the table, not far from clusters of intrigued women making headscarves or mending tunics.

"Would you prefer to sit at the head?" whispered Luke. He was thinking of status. He was thinking of the proper place for a princess to be.

"I would prefer to sit where I may hear everyone who wishes to speak," I answered. A few women smiled triumphantly, as though they approved of putting men-folk in their place.

Luke hesitated but I was already arranging my skirts. For him to object now would be to make a scene, and that would either lower the villagers' opinions of him—or perhaps of me. He couldn't risk either. He sat down to one side of me, examining the elderly man who pulled up a chair on my other side.

I had travelled our villages often enough that I knew the cripple. His name was Don, and since his horse had broken his thigh 'into a lumpy mess, he might as well show the young-uns how to use a drop spindle' and 'raise kittens into barn cats'.

Some of the others I knew, but those I didn't know I was introduced to. Luke had to listen in if he wanted to hear anything; as a guard he was largely ignored. He shouldn't even be at the table, but he was feeling nervous so I allowed it, and since I allowed it, the others did as well.

"There's talk of rebuilding our wool shops. That what we're here for?" Don asked.

Luke frowned, just a twitch of his lip the others didn't notice. They were watching me.

"Yes," I said, wondering what my mother would say when she heard what I was doing. "You might have heard rightly. But I need experts and craftspeople to make the details work. I need you."

Luke frowned more visibly, as though he didn't like my idea of 'experts', but an unchecked smile spread down the table. A serving woman set down two wooden cups, sanded to a polish, in front of Luke. Rings of water obscured makeshift maps of fields and paddocks scored into the table, and Luke did his best to hide the irritated twitch of his lip. Servants in the keep knew to dry off servingware, but I suspected that here they were made hasty by eagerness to not keep me waiting.

A nasally woman's laugh and a man's rough chortle came through the door, both noises cutting short when they saw the meeting taking place. My brother would have commanded silence, but I did not need to. The pair sat down uneasily at the far edge of the table, and I saw a stable boy sit on the tavern's front steps to warn away anyone else.

"So," I said. "Here is what I have in mind."

If there was one thing we had, it was wool. In particular, we had double-fleeced sheep which yielded a special type of wool which would be highly prized, and therefore highly paid. We would need a lucrative industry when the war was over.

In my talks with merchants, the royal courts they visited wanted handmade heirlooms—things we had done before the war. Fabric swatches of different plaids, necklaces and shawls, socks and stockings, slippers and cloaks and more.

The industry would start at shepherds and farmers growing dye, employ washerwomen, spinners and weavers, seamstresses and craftswomen. And if we made peace with the southern country, we would have silk and cotton to make lace with—and more dyes, and access to the sea. I didn't add that part to the conversation, however, not since that could be years in coming.

It took us three hours to go through the plan, and even then we could have spent three hours on different breeds of sheep alone, particularly after the gentlemen surpassed their second pint of heather-scented pale ale. I called an end to the meeting when the youngest became fussy, my own head light and cloudy despite the attention I had given to drinking slowly.

"We have a long time to plan. For now, we all have a lot to think on. Meet here in a week. Don will preside over the meeting if circumstances bar me from coming, and I will attend the meeting after."

"Beloved Princess, are we then a guild?" Don asked, his soft voice raspy despite the cider he had been drinking.

The table grew quiet to hear my answer.

I looked up and down their faces, flushed with talk and bright with merriment. Some a tad too merry. But, they'd do. They'd have to do. A man elbowed his wife into silence and she glared at him then saw me and her face turned red. I said, "I pronounce you the Textile Guild Founders. Add new members pending a committee approval, where the committee has to be arranged with different members every time."

I intended to leave immediately, but I was not allowed. They wanted to speak with me, and so I remained for the better part of two hours before the last person came to say farewell.

The door burst open while I held the woman's hand. A boy on the cusp of manhood clutched the doorframe with one hand, and held his hand to his chest in the other. Blood dripped from between his fingertips, and with him came the winter winds of war.

"Sutton Village. Mercenaries. Darius Black. Our prince is holding them."

Then the boy fell, and with his collapse, so faltered my heart. I gripped the old woman's hand tighter.

"My brother. Luke, my brother." Terror seized my heart and my brain turned into a muddled puddle as I recalled that last time this message had come, I had lost my sister. A sickening claw raked my stomach, and I dreaded the outcome of the skirmish. If he died, I would be alone. Alone and vulnerable, to more armies than just those belonging to Aurelian Black.

www.ingramcontent.com/pod-product-compliance
Lightning Source LLC
Chambersburg PA
CBHW031712170626
46808CB00005B/1710